THE
BEATRYCE
PROPHECY

THE BEATRYCE PROPHECY

Kate DiCamillo

illustrated by
Sophie Blackall

THORNDIKE PRESS
A part of Gale, a Cengage Company

Thorndike Press® Large Print Striving Reader Collection.

The text of this Large Print edition is unabridged.

Other aspects of the book may vary from the original edition.

Set in 16 pt. Plantin.

LIBRARY OF CONGRESS CIP DATA ON FILE.
CATALOGUING IN PUBLICATION FOR THIS BOOK
IS AVAILABLE FROM THE LIBRARY OF CONGRESS.

ISBN-13: 978-1-4328-9145-9 (hardcover alk. paper)

Published in 2021 by arrangement with Candlewick Press

Printed in Mexico
Print Number : 3   Print Year : 2022

For
Betty Gouff DiCamillo
1923–2009
KD

❧

For
Kate DiCamillo
SB

It is written in the Chronicles of
Sorrowing that one day there will come
a child who will unseat a king.

The prophecy states that this child
will be a girl.

Because of this, the prophecy
has long been ignored.

BOOK
THE
FIRST

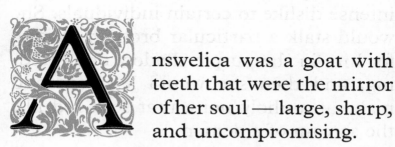nswelica was a goat with teeth that were the mirror of her soul — large, sharp, and uncompromising.

One of the goat's favorite games was to lull the monks of the Order of the Chronicles of Sorrowing into a sense of complacency by arranging her features in a benign and indifferent expression.

For weeks, she would bite no one.

When approached, she would merely stare into the distance as if she were considering something profound. And then, when the brothers had relaxed their guard, thinking that perhaps, somehow, Answelica had changed, the goat would come from behind and butt them in the backside as hard as she was able.

She was very strong, and she had a very hard head. Because of this, the goat was able to send the monks flying great distances through the air.

When they landed, she bit them.

She was a goat who formed peculiar and inexplicable antipathies, taking an intense dislike to certain individuals. She would stalk a particular brother, waiting for him in the purple shadow of a building, and then she would leap out and make an unholy noise that sounded like the scream of a demon.

The monk — terrified, undone — would scream, too.

The monk and the goat would then engage in a duet of screaming until the goat was satisfied and trotted away looking beatific, leaving behind her a trembling, weeping monk.

The brothers of the Order of the Chronicles of Sorrowing would have liked to butcher her, but they were afraid of the ghost of Answelica.

The monks agreed among themselves that the ghost of the goat would surely be more vicious and determined, more impossible to outwit, than the flesh-and-blood goat.

How would she seek her revenge from the afterworld?

It beggared the imagination to consider what the ghost goat would do.

And so she lived.

Which is just as well.

Which is, in fact, wonderful.

Because without the goat, Beatryce surely would have died.

And then where would we be?

Chapter Two ☙

ll of this took place during a time of war.

Sadly, this does not distinguish it from any other time; it was always a time of war.

Brother Edik was the one who found her.

The world that morning was coated in a layer of hoarfrost, and the brother was late to the task of feeding Answelica because he had stood for too long admiring the light of the rising sun shining on the blades of grass and the branches of the trees.

The whole world seemed lit from within.

"Surely, it is evidence of something," Brother Edik said aloud. "Surely, such beauty means something."

14

He stood and looked at the world until the cold made his hands ache and he came at last to his senses.

He trembled as he entered the barn, certain that Answelica — displeased at his lateness — was already plotting against him. But he was surprised to find the goat asleep, her legs folded beneath her, her back to him.

What new ploy was this?

Brother Edik cleared his throat. He put down the bucket. Still, the goat did not move. He stepped closer. He gasped.

His mind was playing tricks on him.

Or rather it was his eye playing tricks — his left eye, which would not stay quiet and still, but rolled around in his head, looking for something it had yet to find.

"Some demon occupies that eye," Brother Edik's father had said, "and that demon has made its way into your mind as well."

And now, in the early-morning gloom of the barn, Brother Edik's wandering eye, his strange mind, was seeing a goat with two heads.

"Have mercy upon us," whispered Brother Edik.

Answelica with one head was already more than the brothers could bear. How could they live with the goat if she had two heads and two sets of teeth?

She would upend the order of the universe. She would put the king from his castle. Answelica with two heads would be a creature capable of ruling the world.

The brother took a tentative step forward. He squinted and saw that the other head belonged to a child curled up beside the goat.

Brother Edik let out a sigh of relief.

And then a new wave of terror engulfed him when he realized that the child had hold of one of the goat's ears.

Chapter Three

child. Next to the goat.

A child curled up and holding on to the demon Answelica!

Brother Edik's heart thumped with dread. The goat's terrible teeth flashed through his mind. He knew those teeth more intimately than he would wish.

On a summer day the year before, Brother Edik had spent what seemed an eternity being chased by Answelica through a flower-studded meadow.

What the goat was doing in this meadow, miles from the monastery, close to the castle of the king, was a mystery that Brother Edik had never solved.

Brother Edik should not have been there himself. It was only that a traveler had told him of the flowers in the field, of their glory and profusion, and Brother Edik thought that he must see this beauty for himself.

In the meadow, the goat had come up behind him, silently, stealthily. She breathed her terrible breath upon his backside; then she gave him a gentle, almost playful, butt with her head.

Brother Edik began to run.

He ran, and the goat followed him. The two of them ran together through the field of flowers. And when, at last and inevitably, Brother Edik tripped and fell, Answelica came up to him and stood with one cloven hoof on his chest, looked deep into his eyes, and opened and closed her mouth.

She drooled on him.

She gave him a good amount of time, another eternity, to consider her teeth in every particular, and to consider, too, the atrocities of which he knew them to be capable.

Just when Brother Edik thought that he could bear it no more, the goat pressed her hoof down upon him very,

very hard, then lifted it and walked away from him.

He bore the mark of that afternoon still — the sullen partial outline of a goat's hoof on his chest. The mark would stay there for the rest of his life, a red arrow pointing to his heart.

As if anyone would need help locating Brother Edik's heart!

"Here," he said now. He took a step closer to the goat. "We must be very careful."

The goat ignored him. The small form nestled up against the goat did not stir. Brother Edik saw that the child's feet were bare and covered in blood.

He shivered. Should he go and get help?

"You coward," he heard his father say. "You broken-eyed coward."

And it was true. He was a coward.

But still, he could not walk away and leave this child alone with Answelica. He would have to confront the goat.

"You goat-fearing fool," he heard his father say.

Brother Edik sighed.

He wished his father's voice would leave him alone. He wished it could be silenced once and for all.

Brother Edik gathered his robe and made to climb over the gate and into the goat's domain.

Answelica stood. She emitted a high-pitched noise.

The child sat up, and Brother Edik saw long hair, astonished eyes, a face shaped like a heart.

A girl child.

She was crying.

It was not outraged crying or sorrowful crying. It was the crying of someone who was tired beyond all reckoning, the crying of someone who was trying very hard not to cry.

Tears rolled down her face as she looked into his eyes, both of them — his steady eye and his wild and wandering eye — and did not look away.

Brother Edik looked back at her. He felt his heart shift inside of him.

He felt it open.

"Oh," said Brother Edik.

Answelica let out another high-pitched noise.

"Shhh," said Brother Edik to the goat and the girl. "Shhhh. All will be well. All will be well."

And yet, even as Brother Edik spoke those words, other words, more ominous words, were being spoken not far away.

In the drafty throne room of the king's castle, a soldier bowed before the king and said, "Sire, the woman is secured in the dungeon, as you commanded. But I must tell you that the child is missing. I have searched all of Castle Abelard and its environs. I could not find her."

"What do you mean you could not find her?" said the king.

"I mean, sire, that she is not there. Her body was not there. The girl is gone."

Chapter Four

Answelica stood next to the child in a ferocious, protective pose.

Brother Edik had one leg swung over the gate and one leg still on the ground.

"Please," he said to the goat.

Answelica looked at him, and then she turned and looked at the child, and then she looked back at him. In the dim barn, it was hard to gauge subtleties of emotion, particularly in the eyes of a being who had seldom before evidenced subtleties of any sort, but Brother Edik thought he recognized the flicker in the goat's eye. It was both a light of affection for the child and a light of warning for him.

23

The goat lowered her head in a threatening gesture.

"It is cold," said Brother Edik from atop the gate. "It is very cold. Too cold for a child. I mean her no harm. I only want to help."

The goat and the monk stared at each other. Meanwhile, the child quietly cried.

Outside, the sun rose higher and higher. A wedge of light entered the barn — golden and warm. Dust motes danced in the air.

Beauty, again.

"Let me in," said Brother Edik to the goat. He spoke softly. "You must let me tend to her."

Answelica took one step back.

For what was surely the first time in her life, she retreated.

Brother Edik swung his other leg over the gate. He stepped into the goat's enclosure.

"Are you injured?" he asked the child.

She was young. Not more than ten years old, although it was impossible to tell for certain, dirt- and blood-encrusted as she was.

The girl did not answer him.

"What is your name?" asked Brother Edik.

Tears continued to roll down her cheeks, clearing a path through the dirt.

Brother Edik took a step toward her. Answelica growled. You would not think a goat could growl, but this goat was forever full of surprises.

"Will you let me carry you?" Brother Edik asked.

Again, the child did not answer. Perhaps she could not speak?

Answelica glared at him. She lowered her head. She offered her ear, and the girl took hold of it. The goat stood quietly, head bowed.

"I am going to carry you," said Brother Edik. And then he announced his intentions to the goat: "I am going to carry her."

The child let go of Answelica's ear.

Brother Edik bent and gathered her in his arms. Her skin was hot to the touch. She was burning with fever.

"She is very sick," Brother Edik said to the goat, who was staring up at him. "The first thing we must attempt to do is to bring the fever down. And we must wash her. We must remove the dirt and blood. She has come from some war, I suppose. Do you not think it so?"

Answelica nodded.

Lord help me, thought Brother Edik. *I am conferring with a goat.*

He walked out of the barn and into the light of day carrying the child. The frost had melted. The world no longer shone, but it was very bright.

Answelica was at his heels.

He turned and looked back at her. He saw that the goat's eyes were gentle, full of concern.

Strange world! Impossible world!

Brother Edik felt his heart, light within him, almost as if it were filled with air.

Answelica butted her head against his legs. It was not a warning, but a request: "Go faster. Please hurry. Tend to the child."

Oh, this strange world.

The sun was warm on Brother Edik's face.

This impossible world.

Oh, this strange world
The air was warm, or Brother Edik's
face
This irresistible

Chapter Five

he dreamed.

The tutor held something in his hand, curled in his fist. "It is for Beatryce," he said.

"What is it?" shouted her brothers. "Let us see, let us see!"

"Tap my hand," the tutor told her.

She touched his fingers, and he uncurled them slowly to reveal a strange creature.

"What is it?" she said.

"A seahorse," he said. "A horse of the sea."

"Does it live?" she asked.

"It is dead," the tutor answered her.

She took the seahorse from his hand. It

was light, so light that it felt as if she were holding someone else's dream cupped in her hand.

She admired the seahorse's curled tail, considered his long nose. She turned him over and saw that he had only one eye.

"Is he made so?" she asked. "With only one eye?"

"No," said the tutor. "Some trauma happened, I suppose."

"It's broken!" shouted Asop.

"I want to hold it," said Rowan.

"In a moment," said Beatryce.

Rowan jostled her elbow, and the seahorse fell from her hand.

This happened slowly, so slowly that it seemed as if the seahorse floated through the air, twisting and turning, his one eye appearing and then disappearing — winking at her.

And then there came a flash of light.

A soldier burst into the hall.

The seahorse never reached the ground.

The dream ended before he could complete his fall, and then it began again: the tutor's closed fist, the tutor's long fingers uncurling to reveal the creature, his voice saying, "A seahorse. A horse of the sea."

Then came the word *dead* and the lightness, the weightlessness, of the seahorse in her hand, the creature falling and falling, the soldier bursting in.

The dream repeated. It repeated and never changed.

The seahorse, it seemed, would never do anything but fall.

Beatryce, caught in her fever, captured by her dream, turned from side to side, working to escape.

She sat up and cried out.

Someone put a hand to her forehead.

There was a snuffling sound, warm breath.

She reached out and found the comfort of a densely furred ear.

I must hold on to this, she thought. *There is nothing else to do but to hold on to this.*

And then she was asleep again, delivered back to the dream, delivered back to the tutor's slowly opening fist and to the seahorse falling, falling, falling.

Chapter Six

rother Edik's task in the Order of the Chronicles of Sorrowing was to illuminate.

He made glorious golden letters that began the text of each page of the Chronicles.

It was both a relief and a joy to him to make the letters match the world as he so often saw it: brilliant, luminous. He went to sleep at night with the letters glowing in his mind and woke with them there, too — elegant, intricately formed shapes that shone and shone.

Sometimes, as he worked, the letters revealed some truth to him — a line of prophecy that would repeat in his head until he knew it to be true.

He would then go to Father Caddis and say, "These words were delivered to me as I worked."

Father Caddis would nod and solemnly write the prophecy down so that it could be entered into the great book, and then he would stand and put his hand on Brother Edik's head and speak the words that had been said to all the many prophets of the Order of the Chronicles of Sorrowing who had preceded Brother Edik: "I thank you for your vision. These words will be recorded."

And after, as Brother Edik went through his day, the objects of the world itself glowed — the bowl on the table, the flowers in the field, the hoe propped against the side of the barn.

This glowing must be the product of his wayward, broken eye — his crooked, strange mind. Or that, at least, was the explanation his father would have given.

Whatever the reason, Brother Edik saw beauty everywhere. He painted that beauty into his letters; he listened for the words of truth.

He wished, often, that his letters illuminated a manuscript less grim, less full of beheadings and treachery and war and prophecies of doom and suffering.

Brother Edik was very sick, supremely sick, of war and violence.

Yet it was war and violence that had brought him the child.

Who could understand the world?

"I do not understand," said the king to the soldier.

"Nor do I," said his counselor. "She cannot have just disappeared. She cannot simply have magicked herself away."

"If the prophecies speak of her," said the king to the counselor, "who knows what powers she has."

"Where is the one who was sent to dispatch her?" asked the counselor.

"He, too, is missing," said the soldier.

"Find her," said the counselor. "Find him. Find them both. She must not live. The very kingdom is at stake."

"Yes," said the king. "The kingdom

itself is at stake, for the prophecies say it is so. Do they not?"

"They do," said the counselor. "So say the prophecies."

For a long time, her fever burned so hot that Brother Edik did not know if she would live. He dribbled water in her mouth. He bathed her in cooling herbs. He prayed over her.

The goat watched his every move, her eyes both suspicious and worried.

The whole of the order watched him.

"It is a time of war," said Father Caddis. "There are many in need. We cannot hover over every refugee who wanders our way. We must feed those in need, bless them, and send them on."

"But she is a child," said Brother Edik. "And she is so ill."

"She occupies your mind," said Father Caddis, "and if your mind is occupied, it cannot properly concentrate upon the work you must do, the words you must receive. Also, there is the matter of the goat."

Here, Brother Edik remained silent, for there was nothing to say.

Answelica had installed herself in the monastery, in the sickroom, at the head of the girl's pallet, and she would not be moved. Anyone who attempted to unseat her was attacked.

The goat would bite, snarl, and snap — making very fine use of her terrible teeth. And then, having subdued her attacker, having — more often than not — made him bleed, she would turn back and consider the child.

The look on her face would miraculously transform from malevolence to adoration.

It was terrifying to behold.

When the girl was obviously distressed, when she cried out, Answelica tended to her. She put her head close and offered her ear, and the child took it and was calmed.

"I believe . . ." said Brother Edik to Father Caddis. He cleared his throat. "It is possible, it could be, that the beast has had a change of heart."

"If it is a change, it is an extremely

limited one," said Father Caddis. "And in any case, I do not care if a change has occurred. We are not in the business of saving goats' souls. Another week — that is all I can allow, Brother Edik. Another week, and then the child must go. Ideally, most ideally, the goat would go with her."

Chapter Seven

n those moments when she was awake, she re-membered.

And she did not want to remember.

She thought that if she remembered, she might die. And she had made the decision to live.

So she climbed willfully out of the clutches of the fever and left everything behind her: her brothers, the tutor, the seahorse, and whatever it was that had happened when the seahorse at last hit the floor.

She gave those memories to the fever. She offered the forgetting as a gift, as a way out, a way to survive.

And when the fever broke, when she

woke at last to the real world, she brought only one thing with her — her name.

Beatryce.

It was a small thing to bring, but it was also everything, for it was a name that would appear often in the Chronicles of Sorrowing.

Chapter Eight 🌀

hat she saw when she woke was sunlight streaming through one small window that was up very high.

She was in a narrow room on a mattress of straw. A goat was beside her, and outside the window, there was a bird calling — singing two high, sweet notes over and over again.

She lay and listened to the bird sing.

She allowed herself to think that the bird was searching for her, singing her name.

Beatryce.

Beatryce.

Beatryce.

"Listen," she said to the goat. "The bird

39

sings my name. Beatryce is my name, and the bird sings it, does it not?"

The goat stared at her from golden, light-filled eyes.

"Beatryce," said Beatryce. "I am Beatryce."

The goat nodded. Beatryce sat up.

"Surely, you have a name, too." She put her face very close to the goat's. "Massop," she said. "Is your name Massop? Or is it Blechdor?"

The goat gazed at her lovingly.

"Perhaps it is Morelich. Am I right? Are you Morelich?"

The sun streaming in through the small window outlined the hair on the goat's ears. The bird sang.

Beatryce wondered if she was dreaming. If so, it was a pleasant dream.

She put her hand on the goat's head. It was knobby and solid and warm. It seemed real enough. She grabbed hold of one of the goat's ears. She gave it a tug just as the door to the room opened.

A monk entered.

"Oh," he said. He stood unmoving

and stared at her. Or rather, his right eye stared at her, and his left eye wandered of its own accord, looking around the room — at the goat, at Beatryce, at the sunlight and the window.

"Your left eye does as it will," said Beatryce. "It dances in your head."

The monk raised his left hand and covered the roving eye.

"No, no," she said. "I did not mean you should hide it." She smiled at him.

He smiled back. He removed his hand. "I am Brother Edik," he said.

"I am Beatryce."

"Beatryce," he repeated.

And she was glad to hear it, glad to hear him say her name. She felt a wave of relief go through her. It was as if the monk were confirming something.

Yes, her name was Beatryce.

Yes, she existed.

"And the goat?" she asked. "What is the goat's name?"

"She is called Answelica."

"Answelica," said Beatryce. "It is not at all the name I expected."

"What name did you expect?"

"I had settled upon Morelich as the most likely."

"Morelich?"

"Yes."

"Why Morelich?" asked Brother Edik.

"Because she did not answer to Massop," said Beatryce. "Or Blechdor."

Brother Edik smiled at her. She liked his face. She liked his wandering, searching eye. She liked his steady, quiet eye, too.

"You have been very sick," he said to her. "Answelica stayed with you all the while."

"Yes," she said. She remembered the fever, the heat and despair of it. "Where is this? Where am I now?"

"You are with the brothers of the Order of the Chronicles of Sorrowing."

"And what are the Chronicles of Sorrowing?" asked Beatryce.

"The Chronicles tell the story of what has happened and of things that might yet happen, those things which have been prophesied."

"Sorrowing," said Beatryce. The word

was a heavy one. "It does not sound like a happy book, a joyful book."

"Alas," said Brother Edik, "it is not."

"Well, then," said Beatryce, "that is not a book I would care to read."

Brother Edik stared at her. "You would not care to read it?" he said.

His wild eye danced. His other eye remained steady on her face — serious, concerned — and some small bell of warning, some bass note of doom, echoed within Beatryce.

"Who are your people?" Brother Edik asked. "They will want to know that you are alive. They will want you home."

And here, whatever brightness Beatryce had felt disappeared.

Who were her people?

Where was her home?

She could not say. A great black emptiness suddenly yawned inside of her.

It was as if she had been walking down a path and turned to look behind her and found that all the things that should have been there, all the things that *had* been there only a moment ago — the trees, the bushes, the birds, the path itself — had suddenly disappeared.

"I'm Beatryce," she said to Brother Edik. "Beatryce."

It was all she could think to say, all that she knew. She started to cry.

Answelica made a goat noise of comfort. She leaned up against Beatryce, and Beatryce wrapped her arms around the goat's neck and wept.

She wept for something she had lost but could not name.

Brother Edik stepped forward. He put his hand on her head.

I am sorrowing, Beatryce thought. *I am with the brothers of the Order of the Chronicles of Sorrowing, and I am sorrowing.*

This thought — the circular truth of it — made her laugh.

"What is it?" asked Brother Edik. "Why do you laugh?"

"Will you write of this in the Chronicles?" she asked. "Will you say that a girl named Beatryce, who does not know where she came from or who her people are, held on to a goat and sorrowed?"

"Yes," said Brother Edik from above her. "It will be written so."

"As something that happened?" said Beatryce. "Or as something that has yet to happen? Will I become a prophecy?"

"Oh, Beatryce," said Brother Edik.

And in the castle of the king, in the throne room, the counselor reassured the king.

"This is nothing but a small delay, sire," said the counselor.

"It is quite worrisome," said the king. "I have been thinking. What if we have mistaken the prophecy as it was written? What if we have the wrong child?"

"Mistaken, sire? I would remind you that if we had mistaken the prophecy as it was written, if we had misunderstood those great words of wisdom, you would not now be upon the throne."

"True, true," said the king.

"We do not have the wrong child. She is the one of whom the prophecies speak. I am certain of it."

"I would not, though, have her killed," said the king. "I want her brought to me alive. Yes, alive, so that I may question her."

The counselor rubbed his eyes. He sighed. "Very well," he said. "You are king. We will do as you command. We will instruct that she be brought back alive."

Chapter Nine

rother Edik's problems were compounded.

There was a child who was no longer hot with fever, but who did not know who she was or where she belonged.

There was a goat who continued to refuse to be separated from the girl.

And worst of all, the girl — when discussing the Chronicles of Sorrowing — had said, "That is not a book I would care to read."

That is not a book I would care to read.

As if she *could* read.

As if such a thing were possible.

Which, of course, it was not.

But still, a shiver of wonder and fear

went through him at the possibility of a girl who could read.

Only brothers in service to God could read, and also the tutors and scholars who came and studied the prophecies.

And counselors to the king.

And the king himself.

In the whole of the world — from the great sea that Brother Edik had never laid eyes on but knew existed, to the dark mountains that Brother Edik had heard described — there was only a handful of people who could read.

All of them were male.

None of them were female.

It was against the law to teach a girl to read, a woman to write.

It had been so for as long as Brother Edik could remember.

The Chronicles of Sorrowing did not say that it had ever been otherwise.

Surely, the child misspoke.

He heard her voice again — playful, imperious. He heard her say, "That is not a book I would care to read."

His heart thumped against his rib cage.

No, he did not doubt it.

He had not misunderstood.

The child, the girl child, could read.

Chapter Ten

e illuminated the letter *B*. He decorated the letter with a twisty, turning vine that was as green as springtime, as hopeful and insistent as the month of May. He made the *B* itself bright and gold like the sun.

And then he took the letter to her.

He held the *B* in front of his chest and said to Beatryce, "Will you tell me what this shape is?"

She looked at the illuminated letter. She looked at him. She said nothing.

His heart fluttered in relief, and also in a strange sort of disappointment.

She was not, after all, who he had imagined her to be.

Beatryce looked at him for a long moment. "Brother Edik," she said.

"Yes."

"Brother Edik, it is in me that I should not say. I don't know why. But I cannot lie to you. That is the letter *B,* and it is the first letter of my name."

Brother Edik's heart sank.

"If I were to give you a quill and parchment," he said, and he heard his voice tremble, "would you be able to write your name?"

"Yes."

"And what else?" he said.

"What else?"

"What else could you write?"

She gave him a great, grave look. "Anything," said Beatryce. "Any word. All words. Is it right that I have told you?"

"Yes," he said.

She smiled. "Will I work to help you write the history of the world, then? Will I join the brothers in chronicling the sorrowing? I would prefer to tell stories. Stories have joy and surprises in them. Do you know the story of the angel and the horse, and how in some trick of destiny, the angel was given hooves and the horse given wings, and the angel danced upon the roof of the palace with her hooves and so woke the king to good deeds, and the horse flapped his wings and flew from this world to another and did not once look behind him?"

This child!

"I do not know that story," said Brother Edik.

"How could you?" said Beatryce. She laughed. "I made it up just now." She became serious again. "But I could, if you asked me, write it down for you, every word of it."

The *B* in Brother Edik's hands trembled as if it were alive. It leapt from his grasp and fluttered to the ground.

Answelica bent her head and snuffled it.

Beatryce said gently to the goat, "No, my sweet. It is not for eating."

The demon goat being called "my sweet."

The girl being able to read. And write.

It was too much. Too much.

What could he do? It was all beyond him.

Brother Edik stared at the top of Beatryce's head. Her hair was snarled and matted. It needed a comb and brush.

He remembered, suddenly, being a boy and holding his mother's brush. It had been a beautiful thing, made of wood, the handle of it shaped like the tail of a mermaid encrusted with small jewels.

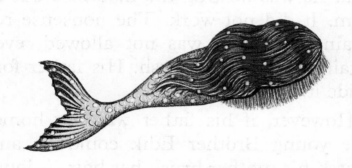

The back of the brush showed the mermaid's head, with the long and flowing curves of her hair, also strewn with jewels.

His father had once caught Brother Edik holding the brush, staring at it openmouthed.

"If she looks this beautiful from behind," the young Brother Edik had said to his father, "then her face must be too beautiful to look upon."

"Whose face?" said his father.

"The mermaid's. If only she would turn and look at me."

His father had become enraged. He told him that he could not stomach the ridiculous notions, the outrageous fancies that the boy's crooked mind conceived of.

His father had beat him. He had said that he was beating the nonsense out of him. It did not work. The nonsense remained, and he was not allowed, ever again, to hold the brush. His father forbade it.

However, if his father was not home, the young Brother Edik could sit and watch his mother brush her hair — long, thoughtful strokes that made the jewels in the mermaid's tail and hair wink and flash.

His mother had beautiful hair. She had told Brother Edik more than once that women were judged for their hair and must work hard to maintain it. "A woman and her hair are one and the same," his mother had said.

"Beatryce," said Brother Edik.

"Yes?"

"I have an idea."

Chapter Eleven

he tried not to think about what she could not remember.

And this, of course, was easy to do. Because she could not remember what she had forgotten, could she?

It is like a riddle, she thought, *a riddle that cannot be solved.*

She could not think about what she had forgotten, but she could think about its great absence, the dark hole where all the knowledge of who she was should be.

For minutes at a time, she forgot this hole, and then she remembered it again, suddenly and terrifyingly — as if some wind had come upon her and caught at her feet and tugged her violently toward the abyss of not-knowing, not-remembering.

She ignored this tug.

She stood very still and let the blackness, the chill of it, pull at her. She stood as firm as she was able, and the feeling passed, and the world — Answelica and Brother Edik and the morning sun and the low murmur of the pigeons on the roof — returned.

She thought about all of this as Brother Edik cut the hair from her head, as she watched the snarled clumps of it fall to the ground.

"Tell me again why my hair must be cut," she said to Brother Edik.

"Because it is too tangled for anything but cutting," said Brother Edik. "There is not a brush or comb in all the kingdom that could find its way through such a snarlsome thicket."

"But there is another reason," said Beatryce.

Brother Edik was silent.

Answelica leaned up against Beatryce's legs.

"What is the other reason?" asked Beatryce.

57

"If you do not fidget," said Brother Edik, "I will give you a moon."

"You have not answered my question," said Beatryce. "And I would like a star this time."

Brother Edik had pieces of maple-sugar candy in the pocket of his robe. The candy was made by Brother Antoine, who shaped the maple sugar into stars and half-moons and leaves and small, grim-faced people.

So far, Beatryce had consumed a moon and a leaf.

Answelica had eaten the people.

"In a moment," said Brother Edik. He leaned toward her. He smelled of maple sugar, and the room smelled of dust and straw. And goat.

Brother Edik cleared his throat. He said, "The world is not always a kind place."

"No," she agreed.

"But there are sweet things to be had," he said.

"Yes," she said.

"I'm cutting your hair so you will be safe."

58

"I don't understand," said Beatryce.

Brother Edik sighed. "My mother," he said, "had a brush in the shape of a mermaid. The mermaid's tail and her hair were encrusted with jewels. The brush was the most beautiful thing I had ever seen, and I wanted something impossible from it: to have the mermaid turn and look at me."

"And did she ever?" said Beatryce.

"She did not."

Beatryce closed her eyes. She imagined the mermaid. She could see her face. It was beautiful and sad.

She opened her eyes again. "What do you suppose the mermaid's name was?"

"I don't know."

"I think it would be important to know her name," she said.

"Maybe you will somehow learn it," said Brother Edik. "I never did."

The sun shone into the room. The odors of goat and maple candy intensified.

Beatryce watched her hair fall to the ground, and she was suddenly filled with a terrible desolation.

59

"Of one thing I am certain," she said to Brother Edik, "and that is that the mermaid did not get her hair cut off."

"No," he said. "I suppose not. But then, she lived in a different world."

Brother Edik bent down and put his face close to hers.

His wandering eye danced around the room, considering everything, while the other eye — bright and steady — looked right at her.

"Beatryce," he said, "when first you told me that you could read and write, you hesitated. You said you felt it was something you should not say."

Beatryce felt the breath of the dark abyss on her neck. She shivered.

"And that was right," said Brother Edik. "It is true that it is something you should not say. In this world we live in, there is a law that states that no girl, no woman, can read or write. You must know this — for your own protection, you must know this."

Beatryce felt herself tip sideways. She took hold of the goat's ear.

"It is very dangerous for you to be who

you are," said Brother Edik. "And so you must pretend to be someone you are not."

"But how can I pretend to be someone I am not when I don't know who I am?"

"You are Beatryce," said Brother Edik. "You know that. You can read and write, and you know that. And this, you must know, too: that you have a true friend named Brother Edik."

Beatryce nodded. "And also a true friend named Answelica," she said. She tugged on Answelica's ear.

"Yes," said Brother Edik. "That, too. So that is who you are: someone with

friends in the world. The rest we will fig-ure out as we go along. I have a plan, and the plan begins with the removal of your hair, even if the mermaid did get to keep hers. Will you trust me?"

She nodded. Her throat felt tight.

Brother Edik nodded in return, and then he went back to work.

Beatryce watched her hair fall to the floor.

She kept hold of Answelica's ear.

She thought: *I am Beatryce. I have friends in the world. I no longer have hair. But I have friends.*

Chapter Twelve

The day after her fever broke and all the hair was cut from her head, the brothers of the Order of the Chronicles of Sorrowing gathered and watched Beatryce — clothed in a monk's robe, her head shaved, a goat at her side — take a quill in her hand and bend over a piece of parchment.

The brothers watched her write.

They watched her form letter after letter.

When she was done, Brother Edik held up the parchment so that every brother could see.

There was a deep and sustained murmuring among the monks.

"How could a girl do such a thing? It

must be some sort of bewitching," said Brother Antoine.

"The letters are perfect," said Brother Adell, "as if an angel had formed them."

"Consider the goat," said Brother Frederik. "The goat is always with her. Does that demon have something to do with this?"

"I would have you all listen," said Father Caddis. "This child endangers us. The castle of the king regularly sends its envoys to study the Chronicles of Sorrowing. What if they discover her? What then?"

"She is but a child," said Brother Edik.

"She is a very dangerous child," said Father Caddis. "And surely, someone is looking for her."

"But we can keep her hidden in plain sight," said Brother Edik. "We will say she is mute. We will say she is a young boy of the nobility come to learn his letters, a brother in training. And in the meantime, she can help us. She can write of the happenings of the world. There are never enough of us for this work. Let her help. This will give her a chance to return to her full health and strength before we send her away. Let us show her some mercy."

Never in his life had Brother Edik made such a long, impassioned speech.

Never before had he stood before his brethren and made such an outrageous request.

But then, never before had anyone mattered so much to him.

Beatryce squared her shoulders. She laid her hand on Answelica's head.

"Just for a short time," said Brother Edik. "Until she is well."

Answelica slowly moved her head, looking each of the monks in the eye.

The goat terrified them all into silence.

She terrified them into agreeing that Beatryce could stay.

And what, you may well wonder, had Beatryce written?

What words had she put down upon the parchment?

These:

> We shall all, in the end,
> be led to where we belong.
> We shall all, in the end,
> find our way home.

When they were alone, Brother Edik asked Beatryce where the words she had written had come from, what text they belonged to.

"I do not know," said Beatryce. "They were in my head, and I wrote them down. That is all I know."

The lines of text were a mystery to her, something hidden inside of her. As she was writing, she had felt the words unfurl from within her one by one and land, bright and beautiful, on the page.

When she had held the quill in her hand, Beatryce still did not know who her people were or where she had come from, but she knew who she was.

66

"Read me the words as they are written in that great book," said the king.

The counselor bent his head to a piece of parchment. He said, "These words are written in the Chronicles of Sorrowing. I have copied them just as they appear. 'There will one day come a girl child who will unseat a king.'"

"Read it entire," said the king.

" 'There will one day come a girl child who will unseat a king and bring about a great change.'"

"Yes," said the king. "But it is a prophecy. Does that not mean it is destined to come true? Should we interfere with fate?"

"Do not doubt," said the counselor. "Small men doubt. Kings do not doubt. And you are a king."

"I will question this child when she is found. For I am king. And that is a thing also written in the Chronicles of Sorrowing — that I was destined to be king."

"Yes, Your Majesty," said the counselor. "That is exactly right."

The counselor allowed himself a small, twisted smile.

His dark robes gave off an oily sheen in the light from the candles that flickered around the throne of the king.

BOOK
THE
SECOND

Chapter Thirteen

ack Dory belonged to no one.

He had come from the dark woods when he was very young.

This, of course, was during a time of war.

The boy had walked into the village alone and said his name to the first person he encountered.

That person was Granny Bibspeak. She was sitting on a stool with her back against her hut and her ancient face turned up to the sun.

Bees hummed. The grass was high and the sky was very blue, blue enough to break your heart in two.

Granny Bibspeak had been in the world

long enough that her own heart had been broken in two any number of times, and she was tired of it. She intended, in the little time that was left to her, to protect her heart.

And so she kept her eyes closed to the beautiful blue and concentrated on the warmth of the sun, the hum of the bees.

When the boy spoke to her, she did not move.

"I am Jack Dory!" the boy said.

"What if you are?" said Granny Bibspeak without lowering her head or opening her eyes.

"There are robbers in the woods," said Jack Dory.

"'Course there are," said Granny Bibspeak. "Them is the dark woods. Filled with robbers, is the dark woods."

"We were going from Highflint to Throttletown," said Jack Dory. "My father did not want to fight in the war, and so we were going from Highflint to Throttletown to avoid the king's men."

To this, Granny Bibspeak said nothing. That people went from one place to another to avoid the wars and the king's men was not news to her, and it was not interesting. In fact, it made her weary to consider it — the constant need of people to run from one thing to another, thinking that they would avoid some sorrow, when sorrow was waiting for them no matter where they went.

Granny Bibspeak was done with such foolishness. She had given up all her illusions. There was no way to be safe in this world, and Granny Bibspeak knew it. She was staying where she was. Let the sorrow come. Let it go past her.

"They stopped us," said Jack Dory, "and the biggest of them had a black beard and a bright knife, and he kept the knife between his teeth, and he growled when he spoke. He sounded like the devil himself."

"So you say," said Granny Bibspeak.

"He took everything from us. He took my mother's cloak. He took my father's hat."

"That's robbers for you," said Granny Bibspeak, still with her eyes closed. "They rob."

"But my father did not like it. He fought

them and they killed him. The man with the black beard killed my father."

Granny Bibspeak felt a pinch in her heart. She wanted to forget the terrible things humans could do to one another. She wanted to sit in the sunshine and listen to the bees and forget.

She did not want to care.

Granny Bibspeak sighed. She opened her eyes. She lowered her head.

She looked at the boy.

Jack Dory.

He was very small. His hair was dark.

"And your mother?" she said, asking the question she did not want to ask.

"She told me to run," said Jack Dory. "She shouted at me that I should run."

"And you did run," said Granny Bibspeak.

"I did. I ran as fast as I have ever run, and I am a very fast runner. I did not look behind me even when I heard her scream, and now I am lost. I do not know where I am, and I do not know where my mother is, and she screamed and I did not turn back."

"Come," said Granny Bibspeak. She held out her hands.

The boy stepped closer to her. Granny Bibspeak put her palms on either side of his face.

"Say your name to me again," she said.

"Jack Dory."

"Aye," said Granny Bibspeak. "Say it again."

"Jack Dory."

"Tell me again who you are."

"I am Jack Dory."

The boy stood with the old woman in the bright sun under the blue sky.

The bees hummed, and Granny Bibspeak made him say his name until he understood somewhere deep inside of him what she was trying to tell him — that his parents were gone, dead, but that he himself still lived.

"I am Jack Dory," he said.

"Aye," said Granny Bibspeak. "You are."

Chapter Fourteen ❦

ranny Bibspeak called him Jack-of-the-Door and Jack-of-the-Wisp. She called him her brave boy. She called him the light of her heart, the river of her soul, her beloved.

She lived for four more years, until Jack Dory was twelve years old, and then she died, and he stayed on in the hut alone. He cared for himself.

He was fast, and because no one had a horse, someone who was fast was prized. He carried parcels. He carried messages.

His memory was prodigious. You could tell Jack Dory something once and it was in his head word for word, just as you had said it to him. In a world where people could not read or write, this memory was a precious thing.

In addition, he had a talent for mimicry. He could make the sound of a wolf calling for another wolf or a raven announcing that it had found food. He could walk like the innkeeper's wife and laugh the same as the blacksmith laughed — before the man had been called to war.

The villagers asked him to tell the old stories, because he could do the voices of all the characters, and it was like watching a play. It was as if they were hearing the story anew.

Because of these talents — because he was fleet of foot and prodigious of memory and a great mimic — Jack Dory wanted for nothing. He was given food and warm clothes. He belonged to no one and was loved by all.

And yet, at night, he dreamed terrible dreams. He dreamed of the bearded robber who had killed his father and his mother. The robber grinned, the knife held between his teeth.

In his dreams, Jack Dory heard his mother scream.

And he awoke, sweating, with one thought in his head: *I want that knife. I will someday have that knife from between the robber's teeth.*

Chapter Fifteen

n the same village as Jack Dory, not far from where the boy dreamed of a knife and revenge, there was a soldier of the king who was abed at the inn.

The soldier was not a young man, nor was he old, and he was terribly feverish, extremely unwell. In the depth of his sickness, at the height of his suffering, it happened that he was visited by an angel — a terrible angel, an angel with dark and ragged wings.

The angel hovered at the foot of the soldier's bed and flapped her black wings. A foul odor rose from the feathers.

"I know who you are," said the soldier. "I have seen you many times on the field of battle. I know that I am now going to die. I want to die! I cannot bear to live anymore."

The angel opened her mouth and closed it again. Her teeth were hideous — crooked, snaggled, and stained.

"What?" shouted the soldier. "What is it that you want to say?"

"You must," said the angel. And then she fell silent.

"I must? I must? I must what?"

"It must be written down," said the angel. "If it is written, then there will be a chance of forgiveness."

"Forgiveness?" said the soldier. "How could I ever be forgiven?"

"See that it is written," said the angel, and then she flapped her malodorous wings and rose up and disappeared through the roof of the inn.

The soldier tried to forget the angel, tried to make himself believe that he had only imagined her, but he could not, and so he got out of the bed and made his way down the dark, crooked, and extremely treacherous stairs of the inn.

At the bottom of the stairs, by the great stone fireplace, the soldier stood as straight as he was able and addressed the innkeeper's wife.

He said, "I am in need of a brother from the monastery."

"You are, are you?" said the innkeeper's wife.

"The angel says it must be written down," said the soldier.

The woman turned from tending the fire to stare at him. "The angel says it?"

"Aye," said the soldier. "If it is written down, I will be forgiven."

"Ha," said the innkeeper's wife. "Forgiveness!" She turned back to the fire.

"Send me a monk!" said the soldier.

"I'm not sending you nothing, am I? But Jack Dory would take a message to them, if you was to pay him."

"Find me Jack Dory, then," said the soldier. "I am ready for this to end. I can bear it no more."

"It will all end soon enough, I reckon," said the innkeeper's wife.

The soldier suddenly felt too weak to stand.

"I must sit," he said.

"Well, sit, then," said the innkeeper's wife.

"There is no chair," said the soldier. But even as he voiced this protest, his legs buckled and he was on the floor.

The innkeeper's wife went to the door and shouted, "Jack Dory! I have a job for you!"

In no time at all, a young boy appeared in the kitchen. He had a great shock of dark hair, and he was smiling.

"This one," said the innkeeper's wife, "this one, sitting on the floor — this one says that he is receiving visits from angels. He wants things written down."

"*I* do not want them written down," said the soldier. "The angel wants them written."

"Take him up to his room," said the innkeeper's wife.

"I can walk," said the soldier. He tried to stand but could not.

"Should I carry you, then?" said the boy.

"You should not," said the soldier. "You could not."

"Aye, sure I can," said Jack Dory. He bent and gathered the man in his arms and made his way up the stairs. He held the soldier as if he weighed no more than a bag of turnips.

The man wished suddenly that he *were* a bag of turnips, for that way he would have no soul to account for, no sins for which to atone. Turnips were blameless, guilty of nothing but being turnips.

No angel of death would bother to visit a turnip and speak of forgiveness and the need to write things down.

"I wish I were a turnip," said the soldier.

"Ah, now, it's not as bad as that," said the boy. He started to whistle a happy tune.

"I have been promised forgiveness," said the soldier.

"Forgiveness?" said the boy. "That's a nice promise."

And then he went back to whistling.

Chapter Sixteen ❧❧

nd so it was that Jack Dory made his way to the monastery, to the Order of the Chronicles of Sorrowing.

When he arrived, he was greeted by a she-goat. She came racing toward him with her head lowered.

Jack Dory had never before seen a goat run so fast. He took a moment to admire her.

Yes, she was very fast indeed.

He let her come toward him, and then at the last possible moment, he took a small, elegant step to the side, and the goat went running past him, still at full speed, on into a field.

He heard laughter, and then a clear

voice said, "You outwitted her. I did not know she could be outwitted."

He turned and saw a robed and hooded figure.

"Aye, I outstepped her *and* I outwitted her. And I could outrun her, too, I'm sure," said Jack Dory.

Just as he spoke those words, the goat returned and butted him in the backside, and Jack Dory went flying through the air.

He flew for some good distance, and when he landed, he put his hands behind his head and lay in the field and looked up at the blue sky and whistled. He pretended that it was what he had intended all along — to relax in a field, whistling and staring up at the sky.

The robed figure stood and laughed, and the goat came to Jack Dory and bent over him and snuffled his hair.

"Hello," he said to the goat. He sat up. "You might want to know that I have come in peace. I have come to fetch a monk to write down a man's confessions. The man is dying, and he has been visited by an angel. This man is a soldier, and he is willing to pay a handsome sum to unburden himself of his sins."

"Why does this man, this soldier, not just say what he has done wrong?" asked the robed figure.

"I am speaking with the goat," said Jack Dory.

"You are wasting your time. She listens to no one but me."

Jack Dory sat up. "And who are you?"

"Her name is Answelica."

"Not the goat," said Jack Dory. "You."

"I am not supposed to say who I am. I am not supposed to talk at all."

"Why?" asked Jack Dory.

There followed a long silence. The goat named Answelica stared at Jack Dory out of her yellow eyes. The wind moved through the field. A bird sang.

Jack Dory waited. He was good at waiting.

"What is *your* name?" asked the small monk.

"Me? I'm Jack Dory."

"Jack Dory, I will tell you a secret."

"No, thank you," said Jack Dory.

"What do you mean?"

"I mean I do not want to know a secret. Secrets are trouble. Granny Bibspeak was forever telling me that secrets are trouble and that trouble has a very long tail."

"Who is Granny Bibspeak?"

"She was the person who loved me," said Jack Dory. "Now, I am here to find a monk to write down what this man says, so he may have some forgiveness. Will you help me?"

"I am Beatryce," the monk said. She pushed back the hood of the robe to reveal a heart-shaped face and a head entirely without hair. She gave him a look of utter defiance. "And I could do it," she said. "I could write what the soldier needs written."

"You?" said Jack Dory. "You couldn't write a thing. You're naught but a girl, a girl without hair."

"You're making me angry," said the girl.

The goat went and stood beside her.

"Look how afraid I am," said Jack Dory.

He stood up and spread his arms wide. "Look how I tremble so." He smiled. He whistled a small song. He looked the girl — Beatryce, it was — in the eye, and then he looked beyond her to the blue sky.

It was a sky blue enough to break your heart in two. He knew that blue. It was the blue of unexpected happenings.

He did not trust that blue at all.

"Will you lead me to a monk who can write the man's words for him, or will you not?" Jack Dory said.

"You don't know me," said Beatryce.

"Aye," said Jack Dory. "I do not."

The goat trotted over to him. She leaned in close, sniffing him. Canny goat, clever goat.

Jack Dory leaned down so that he was face-to-face with her. He wanted to make it clear that he was not the type of person to be pushed around by a goat.

He was staring deep into her yellow eyes when the goat drew back her head and slammed it into his with a sudden, terrible force.

The pain was tremendous. There were

stars dancing inside of Jack Dory's head, and there were bells ringing somewhere, too.

Stars and bells. Bells and stars.

He thought that perhaps he would sit back down again, and so he did.

From what seemed a long way away, he heard the girl — the bald girl in a monk's robe, the girl who said she could write, the girl named Beatryce — laughing.

Chapter Seventeen

She should not have told him that she could write.

She should not have spoken at all.

Brother Edik would despair of her.

But she liked the boy. More, she trusted him.

She did not know why; she just did.

She extended her hand to him. "Here," she said, "take hold of my hand. Your head will stop ringing in a bit. You're lucky she did not bite you. Usually, she bites. The brothers believe that Answelica is a demon. She has attacked them all. She has attacked everyone except me."

Jack Dory took her hand. She pulled him to his feet. He seemed to weigh nothing at all.

"You are as light as air," she said.

"Aye, it makes me fast. I am the fastest person you will ever meet. I am faster even than your demon goat."

"No one is faster than Answelica," said Beatryce.

"I could race her and win easily," said Jack Dory.

"I doubt it most sincerely," said Beatryce.

They walked together through the field to the monastery. Answelica walked between them.

The goat looked up at Beatryce and then over at Jack Dory as if to say, "Did I not send this one flying through the air? Did I not make his head ring like a bell? Who is the most remarkable goat that has ever lived? Tell me."

Beatryce took hold of Answelica's left ear and gave it a tug.

In return, Answelica butted her head gently against Beatryce's leg.

Beatryce had the sudden thought that she had walked before through a sun-drenched field under a blue sky alongside a boy and a goat.

But surely, this could not have happened before. It was only that she was happy — happy with Jack Dory, happy with Answelica.

"Where do you live?" she asked Jack Dory.

"In Granny Bibspeak's hut, in the village."

"Granny Bibspeak," said Beatryce. "She is the one who loves you."

"Aye, loved me. She is gone now."

"Gone where?"

"She died."

"But who cares for you, then?"

"I care for myself."

"What about your parents?"

"Dead," said Jack Dory.

A strange, curled creature flashed through Beatryce's mind. The thing was bright, as if it were made of light, and it was turning, turning.

Seeing it, she stumbled.

Jack Dory reached out and took hold of her elbow. He steadied her. He looked her in the eye. "Truly now," he said, "can you write?"

"You can tell nobody," said Beatryce. "I should not have told you."

"But you can write?"

"Yes," said Beatryce.

"How?"

"I do not know," she said. "I know nothing. I remember nothing. Only my name, just my name."

"Beatryce," said Jack Dory.

"Beatryce," she said in return.

And then Brother Edik was coming toward them. His face was worried, and his errant eye was rolling wildly in his head.

"Who are you?" he asked.

"He is Jack Dory," said Beatryce, "and he is almost, but not quite, as clever as Answelica. His parents are dead. Granny Bibspeak loved him, but she is dead as well. He cares for himself, and he has come to fetch someone to write a soldier's confession. There is money to be had for it. Also, he says that he can run fast, faster even than Answelica." She paused. "And I told him. I told him who I am."

"Aye," said Jack Dory. "There is the

truth of it. All of it, or most of it."

He nodded at Brother Edik, and then he stood smiling at both of them.

"Oh, Beatryce," said Brother Edik.

Chapter Eighteen

he request that Jack Dory brought to the monastery was deemed by all the monks — excepting Brother Edik — to be the perfect solution to the problem of Beatryce.

Was this not what they had prayed for? A way to rid themselves of her?

It was.

They would send her to the inn, to the soldier who needed something written. They would send the goat with her, and they would be done with the demon girl and the demon goat in one fell swoop.

"But how can we send her into the world alone?" said Brother Edik.

"The gold the man gives her will ease her passage through the world," said

97

Father Caddis. "She will find her way. Do not forget that her presence endangers us. Surely, someone is searching for her. Eventually, they will find their way here. And then what? She must go. She must go and not return."

"She is a child," said Brother Edik.

"Do as I say," said Father Caddis. His voice became hard, certain. "Outfit her with a quill and ink and parchment and send her with the boy. I will tell him that he should not bring her back to us. I will tell him that he cannot, under any circumstances, bring her back. The goat must go, too, of course. Providence has provided us with a solution, a way out and through. This is as it should be, as it must be."

And so Brother Edik, coward that he was, did as Father Caddis commanded. He filled a satchel with the necessary instruments of writing, along with a candle and a piece of flint. He also put in the bag as many maple candies as he could find.

As he packed the bag for Beatryce, Brother Edik thought of how he, too, had been sent away as a child, how his father

had delivered him to the monastery and told him never to return.

How could people send their children away?

How did anybody say goodbye to someone they loved?

But that was what the world demanded, wasn't it?

Again and again, the world insisted upon betrayals, goodbyes.

How could anyone bear it?

Chapter Nineteen

ou will go with Jack Dory," said Brother Edik when he handed Beatryce the satchel. "You will write down the words this man says."

"Yes," she said. She took the bag from him. It was heavy in her hands. "And then I will come back to you."

"We do not know what will happen next," said Brother Edik. "Only follow Jack Dory. Do as he says. And do not speak. Truly, Beatryce, it is better if you pretend to be mute."

Beatryce nodded. "I will write this man's confession. I will be as silent as silent can be, and then when I am done with his words, I will write something better. I will write the story of your mermaid."

"How do you mean?" said Brother Edik.

"I mean that I will tell the story of her jeweled tail and her beautiful face. I will tell you what became of her."

She had meant to cheer him, but he was crying.

"Brother Edik?" she said. "Do you not want the story of your mermaid?"

"Yes," he said. He wiped at his eyes. "I do."

"Then I promise I will tell it to you when I return." She looked into his sad eye, the crooked one, the eye that would not be still.

She loved that eye. It seemed to her that it was an eye much better suited than any regular eye for observing the crooked and off-kilter world they all inhabited.

Brother Edik smiled at her. She knew that he did not want to smile, but he smiled for her.

"We will find each other," she said.

"Yes, Beatryce," he said. "We will find each other."

They were three: Jack Dory, Beatryce, and a goat.

Jack Dory did cartwheels as he walked down the road. He followed the cart-wheels with several handsprings.

"You cannot do this, can you?" he said, calling back to Beatryce.

"I cannot do it because I must walk along and pretend to be a monk," said Beatryce.

The satchel was slung across her chest. It bumped against her hip as she walked. Her heart felt heavy.

But the goat did not seem worried. Answelica ran to Jack Dory, kicking up her heels and shaking her head, and then she ran back again and walked at a sedate pace beside Beatryce.

Jack Dory started to whistle a jaunty song.

Beatryce looked down at the goat. She said, "I think he pretends to be happy. I think that deep inside he is sad. Those he loves are dead. He is alone in the world."

Answelica looked up at her, listening.

102

"I am not afraid," Beatryce said to the goat. "I will not be afraid."

Answelica nodded.

She bumped her head against Beatryce's leg. Beatryce took hold of her ear.

"I am not afraid at all," said Beatryce again.

Chapter Twenty

ut she was afraid.

It was so very dark in the room at the inn.

"This? This is the creature who will write my confession? Have you brought me the tiniest monk in the world?" said the soldier.

He was in the bed, the covers pulled up to his chin. His face was red and dotted with sweat and pustules. His hands trembled.

"Why, it does not even look large enough to be a person. Perhaps it is nothing but a robe that you have arranged in the shape of a monk to trick my failing eyes, my failing heart. The world is going dark and you bring me a tiny monk."

"I have brought you what you asked for:

a monk who will write exactly what you say," said Jack Dory. "You did not say what size monk I should bring."

"Speak, you!" said the soldier to Beatryce.

"This monk is mute," said Jack Dory.

"I smell goat," said the soldier.

"You are imagining things," said Jack Dory.

"Never mind. Never mind. It does not matter. Nothing matters now. Leave, boy. And you, tiny little monk, do not look at me. Turn your eyes away from me."

Beatryce lowered her head. She had no desire to look at the man in any case. He was so angry. And he smelled horrible. The whole room stank as if it concealed something dead.

She closed her eyes. She thought of good things, sweet things.

She thought of Brother Antoine's maple candy. She thought of the great golden *B* that Brother Edik had made for her. She thought of Brother Edik's mermaid and the jewels that were strewn through her hair and encrusted upon her tail.

She thought of sunlight streaming through the small window of the room at the monastery.

She thought of Answelica butting Jack Dory so that he flew through the air.

She thought of the surprised look on Jack Dory's face.

Yes, that was a lovely thing to think upon.

She put out her hand and there was the goat next to her, her bony head as solid and warm as a stone on a summer afternoon.

Beatryce opened her eyes.

"I will go now," said Jack Dory.

Stay, please stay, she wanted to say to him. But she did not say it. Instead, she nodded, and Jack Dory nodded at her in return.

And then he leaned close and in a very quiet voice, he said one word to her: "Beatryce."

Only that one word. Her name.

It was as if he were reminding her who she was.

And then he was gone, and it was just

Beatryce and the soldier and Answelica in a dark room on the upper story of an inn, in a village beside a dark wood, not far from a monastery, near a castle where a counselor spoke to a king.

"Soldiers have been sent out across the land, sire. It is only a matter of time until she is found."

"Do you remember," said the king, "when you came to me and took me to the monastery and showed me the prophecy as it was written in the great book?"

"I do," said the counselor.

"Wondrous day," said the king. "I was lost and wandering. I did not know, I would never have dreamed, that such words of prophecy had been written about me. I thought I would lead an un-remarkable life. But instead, I am in the seat of power, in the certain hand of fate."

"It is so," said the counselor.

"Those words that were written about me . . . will you now say them?"

The counselor cleared his throat. "The

youngest son of a youngest son will, against all odds, ascend to the throne."

"Yes," said the king in a voice filled with wonder. "Against all odds. And that was me."

"It was. And it did come to pass. With some assistance."

"Because we must act to make our fate come true," said the king.

"Yes, sire. As I have said: The prophecies are to be heeded. And we are also to act upon them. We will find this girl."

Chapter Twenty-One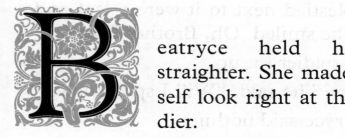

eatryce held herself straighter. She made herself look right at the soldier.

"Look away from me!" he said.

Answelica walked closer to the bed. Her hooves sounded an ominous rhythm on the wooden floor.

"What is that?" said the man. "What evil approaches me?"

The goat put her face right in the face of the soldier, and he screamed.

"Demon!" he shouted.

Beatryce stifled a laugh. She opened the satchel and retrieved the parchment and spread it on the floor. There was no table.

She lit the candle. She readied the ink.

Answelica leaned over and snuffled Beatryce's shoulder. She stuck her head in the satchel and made a noise of delight. The smell of maple rose into the room.

Beatryce pushed the goat aside. She felt in the bag and found a small maple person. Nestled next to it were a leaf and a star. She smiled. Oh, Brother Edik.

The soldier sat up.

"Now?" he said. "Will I speak now?"

Beatryce said nothing.

"I smell goat," said the man. He lay back down. "But who cares? The smell of goat is nothing compared to the terrible stench of the angel. And so I will confess."

The room was silent then and, even with the light from the candle, too dark. The darkness and silence felt familiar to Beatryce. It was the same as the abyss — that terrible place of not-remembering. She felt that emptiness at her back, pushing against her, breathing against her neck.

I will not go, she told herself. *I will stay here.*

She put out her hand and touched Answelica, and it was as if she had cast an anchor for herself in a dark and fast-moving river.

Beatryce steadied. She stayed.

"I will begin!" shouted the man. "I will say it and you will write it, and it will all be done."

Beatryce bent her head to the parchment.

This man would do what he had to do. He would say what he had to say, and she, too, would do what she had to do. She would write it down. And then she and Answelica would go back to the world — back to Jack Dory and Brother Edik, to the sunlight and the fields.

The soldier cleared his throat.

From outside, there came the sound of birdsong — a single note, high and bright.

After a long pause, the bird called out again. And then it sang a song, a song of happiness and sadness, lightness and darkness.

What kind of bird could it be? What kind of bird sang such a complicated, heartbroken, and beautiful song?

Beatryce raised her head. She listened. And then she understood.

It was Jack Dory.

Her heart flooded with light. He wanted her to know that he was there, close by, and that she was not alone. She smiled.

It made a great deal of sense to her that Jack Dory would pretend to be a bird. He moved through the world with the same lightness.

She remembered, again, him saying her name before he left the room.

Beatryce.

"I am Beatryce," she whispered to herself. She put a piece of maple candy in her mouth. The sweetness of it blossomed inside of her.

"I have killed," said the man.

And with those three words, all thoughts of birds and songs and sweetness went out of Beatryce's head.

Her heart became heavy, filled with dread.

"How many have I killed?" said the man. "I do not know. Write down that I have taken life after life, too many lives to count. There were wars and I fought in them as a soldier should, as a soldier must. And then there were those killings that I did at the king's request, specifically at the king's request. And I did it all without regret. Yes, without regret!"

Beatryce felt the room tip sideways and then right itself again.

She dropped the quill and reached for Answelica's ear.

"Are you writing it down?" shouted the man. "Write it down!"

But she did not want to write it down. Who would want to write such terrible words?

"Write it!" shouted the soldier.

Beatryce let go of the goat's ear. She picked up the quill. She dipped it into the pot of ink. She wrote, *I have killed.* Her hand trembled.

"I regret *almost* none of it," said the soldier. "I regret the children. That is surely what the angel wants recorded. I regret the children."

Beatryce looked up. She held herself very still.

"Two boys and a girl. I killed them. Write that down."

But Beatryce could not write. She could not move. Some paralysis afflicted her. She stared into the candle flame and saw a creature curled and glowing.

What is it?

A seahorse. A horse of the sea.

Seahorse, seahorse, horse of the sea.

And then, suddenly, the creature was tumbling through the darkness, away from her.

Beatryce put her hands over her eyes. She lowered her head to the floor.

The man was crying now — loud, ragged sobs.

Answelica butted Beatryce very gently.

Beatryce lifted her head and took her hands from her eyes and saw the goat.

"Here," the goat seemed to say, "here. Stay here."

And then the soldier said, "Under this bed is the sword. It is the sword that did the deed. I cannot get it clean. It will not come clean."

These words seemed to come from very far away.

Answelica butted her head against Beatryce again.

Stay. Stay here.

And Beatryce remembered then that she had promised Brother Edik she would tell the story of the mermaid.

The mermaid.

Beatryce bent again to the parchment. She crossed out the words *I have killed.*

She wrote, *Once, there was a mermaid.*

Chapter Twenty-Two

ack Dory sat under the eaves of Granny Bibspeak's hut. He tipped his stool back and leaned against the warm wall and put his face to the sun. He closed his eyes.

He imagined Beatryce in the dark room. He imagined her writing.

A girl who could write! It was unbelievable, strange.

And also very dangerous, which was surely why the monks did not want Beatryce brought back to them.

It is dangerous, Jack Dory, he said to himself. *Mark that it is dangerous. Trouble has a very long tail. Aye, this girl must be kept close. She must be protected.*

116

And so he put her in the center of his mind.

Beatryce.

He willed her safe.

Jack Dory knew that you could not keep people safe. Nevertheless, he worked at keeping Beatryce — Beatryce who could write, Beatryce and her goat, Beatryce and her laughter — safe in his mind.

He heard horses' hooves.

He kept his eyes closed and his back against the sun-warmed wall, but his heart beat faster.

Horses were rare things.

Horses belonged only to the king and the king's men, and it could mean nothing good to have a soldier of the king appear in the village when there was a girl in the village who could write.

Trouble has a very long tail.

The horses' hooves came closer, closer. Jack Dory's heart beat faster. And then there came the sound of someone dismounting, the clank of a sword.

Jack Dory thought, *Well, let it begin, then.*

He brought the stool forward. He put his feet on the ground. He opened his eyes.

A soldier of the king was standing before him.

"Boy," said the soldier, "are there strangers abiding in your village?"

"Strangers?" said Jack Dory.

"People unknown to you."

"Ah, people unknown to me. Not a one."

"Nothing is different here?" said the soldier. He had small eyes. He kept his hand on the hilt of his sword.

"Everything is just as it ever was," said Jack Dory. "Not one thing has changed. It is the curse of this little place to stay the same as it has always been." He smiled.

"I will ask again in the clearest terms possible. Has there been a girl child who came to this village alone and looking for shelter?"

Jack Dory's heart fell.

Beatryce.

He looked into the eyes of the soldier.

There was no light in those small eyes, no mercy at all.

"There has not been any sort of a girl who has come here," Jack Dory said without looking away. He willed his heart to beat slowly, slowly.

"Understand, we will ask the question of everyone," said the king's man. "We will knock on every door of every hovel in this village. We will question every soul. To lie would mean death. We are here on a mission for His Majesty himself. It is the king who looks for this girl. Do you understand?"

"I understand," said Jack Dory. "It is the king himself." He smiled.

"This is no laughing matter, boy. The girl is bewitched. She is a danger to herself and to all who encounter her."

"But I am not laughing," said Jack Dory, "am I? And I know no dangerous girl."

"What about a soldier? Have you seen a soldier?"

"A soldier?" said Jack Dory. He kept the smile on his face. "Is that a trick question? I'm seeing a soldier now, am I not?"

"I will search your hut," said the soldier.

"Search all you want," said Jack Dory. He waved his hand in the direction of the door, and then he tipped his stool back again, put his face to the sun, and closed his eyes.

He heard the soldier cross the threshold of Granny Bibspeak's hut and then come back out again. He heard the buzz of a bee and then, finally, the sound of hooves and the jingle of the king's soldier's spurs as he led the horse away.

Jack Dory kept his eyes closed. He waited and then waited some more. The bee hovered companionably near his head.

He had often thought that if Granny Bibspeak bothered to return from the next world — for surely there was a next world, a different world, a world that made more sense than this one — it would be in the form of a bee.

And because of this, Jack Dory spoke to all bees, every bee.

"All is well, Granny Bibspeak," he whispered. "Do not worry. I will do nothing foolish, I promise you." He opened his eyes.

The bee was directly in front of him, humming.

"But never again will I sit idly by," said Jack Dory. "No, nor will I ever again run away. I will not. I promise you."

 lowly, Jack Dory lowered the stool legs to the ground. He stood. He stretched. He said, "We will go and get her now, Granny Bibspeak."

He made his way to the inn.

"Now what?" said the innkeeper's wife. "It is never silent here. Always someone demanding something."

"Aye," said Jack Dory, "then you, too, talked to the soldier of the king."

"Looking for a strange child, he was."

"Did he go upstairs?"

"I told him there was nothing up there but a monk and a dying man. But he had to go see for himself. He came back downstairs quick enough. He said, 'Mother, it

122

smells of death upstairs. And there is a goat. You did not tell me of the goat. The goat is in a very bad mood!' He laughed. I did not laugh with him. There is nothing funny to me about a goat in a bad mood."

"I think I will go and pay that goat a visit," said Jack Dory.

"Do as you please. Everyone else does." She shook her head. "A bewitched girl child. That is who he is searching for. The king wants her, if you can believe such a thing."

Jack Dory *could* believe such a thing, and so he climbed the stairs slowly, afraid of what he might find.

In the dark room, the man was weeping as if he would never stop. The blankets were over his head.

Beatryce was on the floor. She was bent over a piece of parchment, writing and writing.

The goat was beside her. She looked at Beatryce and then at Jack Dory, and then she looked back at Beatryce again as if to say, "You see how it is here."

"I do see," Jack Dory said to the goat.

"Beatryce," he said, and then he remembered that he should not have said her name.

But she did not look up, and the man did not stop crying, and it was as if Jack Dory had not spoken at all.

"Beatryce," he said again in a whisper.

He bent down and took Beatryce by the shoulders and shook her. The goat stuck her head in between them — to intercede or to assist, Jack Dory could not tell which.

She was a very troublesome goat.

Jack Dory was beginning to form a fondness for her.

"We must go," Jack Dory said to Beatryce. He pulled her to her feet, and in doing so, he knocked over the pot of ink. Black ink, dark as blood, spread across the floor.

Beatryce looked at the ink and then up at Jack Dory. She looked past him. She said, "Under the bed there is a sword."

"A sword?" said Jack Dory.

"Under the bed there is a sword," said Beatryce.

It was as if someone had put a spell on

her and "under the bed there is a sword" were the only words that she was capable of speaking.

"Very well," said Jack Dory. "I will look under the bed for a sword." He bent down and reached under the bed and felt something heavy and cold. He pulled the thing out and held it up.

A sword — the blade of it long and terrible and gleaming mutely.

The dark-bearded face of the robber flashed through Jack Dory's mind — the robber and the knife he held between his teeth.

Jack Dory thought that a sword such as this would be a very useful thing to have.

Answelica butted him in the leg.

He looked down at her. "Yes," he said. He lowered the sword. "You are right. We must go now."

The soldier suddenly threw the covers from his head. He shouted, "She returns! Do you see her? She returns!"

"Beatryce," said Jack Dory. "We must go." He pushed her before him out of the room and down the stairs.

The goat followed, her hooves clattering on the wooden steps.

Ahead of them, a bee hovered in the gloom.

"Yes, Granny," whispered Jack Dory, "I have her here. I will keep her safe."

The goat made a noise that seemed to say, "Hurry, hurry, faster."

From the room behind them there came a flash of light and a terrible stench, and then the sound of great wings beating together.

The sword was heavy, menacing — glorious — in Jack Dory's hands.

In the castle, the youngest son of a youngest son, the man who was now king, was being entertained, distracted. He sat upon his throne and clapped in time to the song of the court musicians. He laughed at the court jester. He marveled over the juggling.

And the counselor to the king?

He stood in his dark robes, alone, in the castle keep.

126

He looked out upon the land. From the keep, the counselor could see a long way, a very long way indeed. He could see all the way to Castle Abelard, perched on a cliff and overlooking the sea.

"Here is a question," said the counselor. "Is it better to be the king or to be the man behind the king? That is, is it better to be the puppet or the puppet master? Answer me that question, Beatryce, you who always had an answer for every question. Beatryce of Abelard, can you answer that question for me?"

The counselor smiled his small, twisted smile.

"No need to hurry. I can wait for your answer. I am a patient man. In the meantime, as I wait, perhaps I will go and ask your mother a few questions, too."

BOOK
THE
THIRD

Chapter Twenty-Four

hey went to the dark woods.

The dark woods were not safe, but right now, surely, they would be safer than the village, or so said Jack Dory.

Beatryce did not know or care about the dark woods. She did not know or care about what was safe or not safe. She found herself unwilling to care about anything. Her body was heavy. Her limbs were weak. It felt as if she had been asleep for a thousand years.

There was a story about a man who had been made to sleep for a thousand years. He woke to see that the stars had reconfigured themselves in the sky and that the sun rose in the west instead of the east.

The man called out, "What world is this I now inhabit, and how shall I live in it?"

Someone had told Beatryce that story.

Who?

She could not remember.

She could remember nothing. Nothing.

They went deeper into the dark woods, and it was as if they were entering a great green cave.

What world is this I now inhabit, and how shall I live in it?

When they were entirely surrounded by trees, Jack Dory turned to her and put down the sword. He placed his hands on her shoulders. "Beatryce," he said. "Beatryce."

He shook her gently. "Wake up, now," he said. "You must." He took her hand and placed it on Answelica's head.

"Beatryce," he said, "I need you."

And with these words, and with the goat's warm, solid head beneath her hand, the world came closer. Beatryce felt something turn over in her and start to hum.

She looked into Jack Dory's eyes. He

smiled at her. "There you are. Listen. Listen to me. They are after us. I think we should climb this tree. It is tall enough to see who is coming and it will keep us hidden."

"But what of Answelica?"

"What of her?"

"She cannot climb a tree."

Jack Dory looked down at the goat and smiled. "Most likely not. But then, I would put nothing past her. We will have the goat stay at the base of the tree and guard us. How is that?"

He looked up at the tree. "Should I lift you?" he asked Beatryce.

"You should not," she said. She walked past him and took hold of a low branch and swung herself up into the tree.

"Ha," said Jack Dory. "Someone has taught you to read and write, and someone has taught you, too, how to climb a tree."

He smiled up at her.

"Here," he said. "I will have you hold the sword while I climb."

"No," she said. She felt a terrible shudder

go through her, a great gust of darkness. "I do not want it."

"Take it so that I might have my hands free to climb."

"No," she said again.

Jack Dory sighed. He planted the sword in the earth and swung himself up into the tree and then leaned down and pulled the sword up.

They sat together on the same branch, and Answelica looked up at them, shifting from hoof to hoof. It was as if she were considering how best to go about climbing the tree.

"Stay there," said Beatryce to the goat. "You must guard us."

"Hold the sword and I will go higher," said Jack Dory.

"I will not hold that sword," said Beatryce. "Do not ask me again."

"Very well, then," Jack Dory said. "We will just stay here, exactly where we are. In the dark woods. In the low branches of a tree. Guarded by a goat. Surely, this will come out right. What could possibly go wrong?"

He whistled a few notes.

"I heard you whistle to me," said Beatryce. "Earlier. Before."

"Aye," said Jack Dory. "I did."

"I want to hear that song again," said Beatryce.

"I do not know that I should be whistling at all," said Jack Dory. "They are after us."

"Who?" said Beatryce.

"Soldiers of the king," said Jack Dory. "That is why it is good to have this sword."

"The man said that he killed too many people to count with that sword."

"What else did he confess?" asked Jack Dory.

"I don't remember. I don't want to remember." She felt the dark breath of the abyss on her neck. She shuddered. "Where is Brother Edik? I want to see Brother Edik. I want to go back to the monastery."

"You cannot go back. There is no going back."

Terrible words!

"They are looking for you," said Jack Dory. "The monastery is surely one of the places they will search. It is the king himself who wants you. I don't know why. I expect it is because you can form letters. They say you are bewitched."

What world is this I now inhabit, and how shall I live in it?

The wind blew through the leaves of the tree, and Beatryce felt it blow through her, too, as if she were some hollow thing.

"They are only letters," she said. "It is not witchery. They are letters and words." She looked down at her hands. There were dark places on the thumb and forefinger of her right hand — ink stains.

That is where the words come from, she thought, *those dark places.*

"What else did the man confess to?" asked Jack Dory.

"I said I do not remember. Why must you know everything there is to know? You annoy me."

"Aye, well, and you annoy me in return," said Jack Dory. "After all, it is only because of you that I am hiding up a tree in the dark woods."

Below them, Answelica bleated once, and then again. There came the sound of footsteps. Someone was making their way through the undergrowth.

"Shhh," said Jack Dory.

"Do not tell me to 'shhh,'" whispered Beatryce. "I know very well when to be quiet. I am not some dullard."

"Shhh," Jack Dory said again.

Beatryce rolled her eyes at him and leaned forward. She could see nothing.

A voice said, "Ah, look at this. A goat. A goat. A sweet goat."

And then the voice turned the words into a song:

*"A sweet goat all alone
awaiting me
in the green woods.
Hello, my all alone,
hello, my sweet goat gone
all alone.
Will you come with me,
my sweet goat a-waiting
in the green woods,
will you come a-gallivanting
with me?"*

It was a very pretty song, with a very pretty voice singing it.

When the song ended, there was a small silence. And then came a familiar noise — the sound of Answelica's head meeting a human body with great force.

Both Beatryce and Jack Dory leaned forward.

Someone was flying through the air, someone in robes with long gray hair.

Beatryce could not tell if it was a man or a woman. The robes were gray and the hair was gray, and altogether the creature resembled a spirit more than a human being.

But here was the wonderful thing: whoever they were — man or woman or ghost — they were laughing.

Chapter Twenty-Five

t was a man on the ground.

He was on his back and he was laughing. He pulled his knees up to his chest and laughed and laughed.

At least Jack Dory thought it was laughter. He was not certain. The man seemed to have lost his wits entirely, either to sorrow or joy.

The man's hair was long, and his beard was longer. It came down almost to his knees.

Answelica stood over the man with her head lowered, studying him.

"Ah, goat, goat," sang the man. "Wheeee. Goat, goat, sweet goat, won't you go a-wandering with me? Wheeee."

He sat up and patted Answelica on the

head, and the goat allowed it.

The man wiped his eyes on the sleeve of his robe. He looked up at the tree.

Jack Dory put his hand on Beatryce's shoulder and pulled her back.

"No use in trying to hide," said the man. "I know that you are up there. I can smell both of you. It is a smell I know well; it is a smell even stronger than the smell of goat. You smell of fear."

Jack Dory heard Beatryce's sharp intake of breath.

"You are right to be afraid," said the man. "You cannot go through these woods without encountering great danger. These woods harbor evil. However, I could, were I so inclined, offer you safe passage. My knowledge of these woods is deep and wide."

There came another thud.

Jack Dory and Beatryce leaned forward.

The man was on his back again, rolling around on the forest floor, laughing and laughing. "Or perhaps I will not offer you safe passage," he said, "as your goat — wheee — your goat seems intent on killing me."

"Sir!" said Jack Dory. He rose to standing in the crook of the tree and held the sword out in front of him. "I would advise you to look at what I carry."

"Stop," said Beatryce.

Jack Dory ignored her. He said, "Do you think, sir, that we would come through these woods unprotected? Do you think us fools? We are not fools. I know very well what hides and festers in these woods. I know what evil lives here."

There was a long silence.

Answelica let out a questioning bleat.

"We are protected by the king," said Jack Dory. "We would have you know that we are on royal business. We are, in fact, carrying a message to the king."

"Liar," whispered Beatryce.

Yes, it was a lie. But Jack Dory felt this was a situation for lying. And further, why not make it a clever lie? Why not say that they were running toward the very thing that they were running from?

"We have been entrusted with important words," said Jack Dory, "words upon which the fate of the entire kingdom rests. This monk in the tree with me —

do you see him? This monk is mute, and his growth has been stunted by various and assorted troubles."

Jack Dory was having a fine time now!

Beatryce pinched his leg.

"Ouch," said Jack Dory. "As I was saying, this stunted and deformed monk is a personal scribe to the king, and I must make sure he returns to the king safely. So that the message can be delivered."

The man had stopped laughing. He was standing now and looking up at the two of them, studying them. His face was smooth and unlined, which was disconcerting given the length and color of his beard.

"You have a message for the king?" said the man.

"Aye," said Jack Dory. "We do."

The man began to laugh again. "You have a message for the king, a message — hee-hee-hee — for the king." He bent over and put his hands on his knees. "Oh, stars and saints in heaven above, look down upon me and — hee-hee-hee — laugh with me."

Answelica looked up at Beatryce and

Jack Dory, and then at the laughing man, and then back at them again, as if to say, "Here is a very fine specimen of humanity. Should I send him flying again?"

"He is mad," Jack Dory said to Beatryce.

"I am not stunted," said Beatryce.

"Your temperament is stunted," said Jack Dory.

The man with the beard stopped laughing. He said, "Look here, sooner or later, you will have to come down from that tree. Come down now. I will do you no harm. I promise you. I would not interfere with the — hee-hee-hee, oh, stars and saints above, the irony of it! The sweet irony! — message for the king."

Jack Dory stood in the tree with Beatryce beside him and the goat and the man below him. He stood with the sword in his hand. The birds were singing.

A bee formed lazy circles above his head.

"I believe him," whispered Beatryce.

"I do not believe him," said Jack Dory, and he did not whisper.

"Answelica believes him. See? She has not attacked him again."

"What does it matter what a goat believes?"

"I am leaving," said Beatryce. "You can do as you will." And she started climbing down the tree.

What could Beatryce know about the dark woods?

What could a goat know about whom to trust?

Nothing.

But what choice did Jack Dory have, truly?

None.

Where Beatryce went, he must go.

Somehow that had happened. He was not sure how — but whither she went, so went he.

Jack Dory sighed. He followed Beatryce.

Chapter Twenty-Six

he bearded man led them through the woods.

They went single file behind him: Answelica first, Beatryce behind Answelica, and Jack Dory behind Beatryce.

The goat picked up her legs very high, prancing as if she were the one in charge. She glanced behind her occasionally, looking at Beatryce.

"Are you here, then?" Answelica seemed to say. "Are you with me?"

"Yes," Beatryce answered with her eyes. "I am here."

As for Jack Dory, he was carrying the sword out in front of him, and whenever Beatryce turned and looked behind her, she saw the terrible, gleaming menace of it.

The sword knew something.

The sword had a terrible story that it wanted to tell. But Beatryce did not want to hear that story.

She remembered what Jack Dory had said: the king was looking for her.

The king!

She looked down at her thumb and forefinger, at the smudges of ink there.

Yes, the king was looking for her because she could read and write.

She felt the deep, dark hollow inside of her twist and open.

Who was she?

Answelica, again, looked back at her. Beatryce smiled at the goat.

They walked on.

The woods were green to the point of darkness.

The man with the beard turned suddenly. He said, "I have been in many a procession in my life, but never one as strange as this. I can walk with a goat at my heels, but I cannot walk with a sword at my back. Lower the sword, boy. I assure you that I am not intent on evil."

"Ha," said Jack Dory.

"Lower the sword and tell me your name," said the man.

"His name is Jack Dory," said Beatryce. "And I am Beatryce, and the goat is named Answelica."

"Ah," said the man, "so you are not, after all, a mute monk whose growth has been stunted by various and assorted troubles."

"I am Beatryce," said Beatryce. "Who are you?"

"Who am I? I am someone who gave up his name quite some time ago." The man smiled. He stroked his beard. "In truth, I gave up everything quite some time ago. But you may call me . . . let's see . . . Cannoc. Yes, Cannoc. It is easier, I suppose, to have a name than not."

"Cannoc," said Beatryce.

"Yes," he said.

"Where are you taking us?" asked Jack Dory.

"Lower the sword," said Cannoc, "and I will tell you."

Jack Dory made a sound of disgust. He lowered the sword.

"I am taking you somewhere safe," said Cannoc. "You must trust me."

"My parents died in this wood," said Jack Dory. "I am inclined to trust nothing and no one here."

Cannoc nodded. "Terrible things happen here." He paused. "But then, terrible things happen everywhere."

"Aye," said Jack Dory. "They do."

"We have only a little way to go before we are safe," said Cannoc. "Will you abide with me for just a short while longer?"

"Yes," said Beatryce for both of them, for the three of them.

She trusted the man.

Why?

Because his song about Answelica had been so beautiful. Because he laughed so well.

And why did she trust Jack Dory?

Because of his whistling and cartwheeling. Because he had come for her and taken her from a dark room.

And Brother Edik? She trusted him because of his crooked, wandering eye; his golden letters; and his great gentleness.

And then there was the goat. Beatryce trusted Answelica for the boniness of her head, the softness of her ear, and for her fierce, uncompromising love.

Were these good reasons to trust?

She did not know.

She could only say that she did trust.

"Jack Dory?" said Cannoc.

"Very well," said Jack Dory.

Cannoc nodded. He turned and resumed walking.

Answelica gave Beatryce a grave and knowing look. She turned and followed Cannoc.

Beatryce followed the goat.

And Jack Dory followed Beatryce.

"Cannoc?" said Beatryce. "Perhaps you would sing again? Perhaps you could sing the song about the sweet goat in the green woods?"

Cannoc laughed. "I could sing that song," he said.

And he did.

Chapter Twenty-Seven ❧

ack Dory was right, of course.

The king's soldiers came to the monastery in search of Beatryce. They came that very day. And it did not take them long to learn that the girl had indeed been there and that Brother Edik had been the one to find her.

He wept as they questioned him.

He wept because he was afraid.

But more, he wept because he should have never let her out of his sight. He should have gone with her.

"Listen, you crooked-eyed man," said one of the soldiers. "I will get the whole truth out of you. This child, this girl, she could read and write?"

"Yes," said Brother Edik.

"She is the one, then, whom the king wants," said the soldier. "It is her."

It was here, in this moment, that Brother Edik remembered being a young man, standing before Father Caddis and saying, "These words were given to me."

"Say them," Father Caddis had said.

"There will one day come a girl child who will unseat a king and bring about a great change," said the young Brother Edik.

"Your words will be entered into the Chronicles of Sorrowing," said Father Caddis.

It had been one of Brother Edik's first prophecies, and he had not thought about the words since. But now, suddenly, he understood them.

It was Beatryce.

Those words of prophecy had been about Beatryce.

"Yes," he said, raising his head and looking the soldier in the eye. "She is the one."

The soldiers searched the monastery,

every inch of it, and when at last they had gone, Brother Edik gathered parchment, a quill, a flint, and a candle and put them in a satchel. He heard his father's voice: "Oh, ho! The great soldier prepares for battle!"

"Yes," said Brother Edik to his father, who was not there, who was long dead. "I do."

He went to the kitchen and asked Brother Antoine for a handful of maple candies.

"For the girl?" said Brother Antoine.

Brother Edik nodded.

"You will not find her," said Brother Antoine.

"Perhaps not," said Brother Edik. "But I must try."

Brother Antoine shook his head. "Your task is to illuminate the Chronicles. Your task is to listen for the words of prophecy. It is not for you to intercede. If you leave, Father Caddis will not let you return."

"Nonetheless," said Brother Edik, "I will intercede. At least I will attempt to intercede."

Brother Antoine shook his head again —

slowly, sadly — but he gave Brother Edik all the maple candies in his possession, candies that he had held in reserve for some time: candies in the shape of flowers and birds and leaves and crescent moons and stars and also, of course, candies in the shape of small bewildered people.

He filled the pockets of Brother Edik's robe.

Before he left the monastery, Brother Edik went into the room of the Chronicles of Sorrowing. He looked through the book until he found those words he had spoken when he was young.

There will one day come a girl child who will unseat a king and bring about a great change.

Yes, there they were. Written in Father Caddis's hand.

Brother Edik shook his head in wonder. He picked up the quill and wrote his name and the date beside the prophecy, and then these words:

On this day, I did go in search of the one of whom this prophecy speaks: a child named Beatryce, a girl who can read and write, a child who has caused me (and also a goat named Answelica) to believe in love and tenderness and some greater good.

Next to his words, Brother Edik drew a small illumination.

A mermaid.

And then he walked out of the room of the Chronicles of Sorrowing, out of the monastery, and into a field filled with blooming elderhist. The yellow flowers bowed and brushed against him as he walked past.

"Coward," he heard his father say. "You surely do not have the makings of a soldier. You belong nowhere but with the monks."

"Where I belong," said Brother Edik aloud — to no one, to everyone, to his father, and to the flowers — "is with Beatryce."

He went first to the inn.

And there he found that the man who wanted his confession written was dead, and that Beatryce was, of course, gone.

And that Jack Dory was gone.

And the goat?

Gone also.

On the floor of the room in which they had all been, there was an ink stain that looked like the map of some other kingdom, some other world, a different place entirely.

"And did you see them go?" Brother Edik asked the innkeeper's wife when he raised his eyes from the ink on the floor.

"I know nothing at all," she said. "It does not matter who questions me, I know nothing. Did I watch Jack Dory lead that monk and that goat into the dark woods? I did not. Did I see that Jack Dory held a sword? I did not see it. Did the little monk leave this parchment behind? Not to my knowledge, he did not. I do not know where it came from, do I?"

The innkeeper's wife handed Brother Edik the piece of parchment.

He held it before him and read the words that had been marked through — *I have killed* — and the words that remained:

Once, there was a mermaid.

Once, there was a mermaid.

Once, there was a mermaid.

The same words had been written over and over, again and again.

"I know nothing of anything," said the innkeeper's wife.

"Nor do I," said Brother Edik. "Nor do I know anything of anything. But I thank you."

And so Brother Edik headed to the dark woods, in the direction that the innkeeper's wife had pointed after she told him, again and again, that she knew nothing at all.

It was evening. The sun was setting, sending out long rays of light that set the whole world on fire.

Did he think he would find Beatryce?

He did not know.

But he thought it mattered that he should look for her, that he should never give up searching for her.

Brother Edik walked through the dying light.

156

He thought about the Chronicles of Sorrowing and the small illuminated mermaid who waited in its pages.

Her hair and tail were strewn with jewels.

And her face?

Her face was the face of Beatryce.

Chapter Twenty-Eight

hey were in a tree again.

Not in the branches of a tree, but in the trunk of it. They had walked through a door hewn into the side of a massive tree, and they were inside it now.

For the rest of his life, Jack Dory would remember the wonder of it: what it was like to open a door and enter another world, a world hidden inside of the world he already knew — the impossibility of it, the rightness of it.

Inside, in the snug hollow, there was a rough-hewn table and a chair, a bed among the tree roots, and bearskin rugs on the floor.

"Oh," said Beatryce. "It's beautiful."

"Sit," said the man named Cannoc. He pointed to one of the rugs.

Jack Dory and Beatryce sat.

The goat, however, remained standing. She looked around her suspiciously.

Cannoc gave Beatryce and Jack Dory each a piece of honeycomb.

"Eat," said Cannoc.

"Thank you," said Beatryce, but a moment later, she was asleep, her back against the goat, the uneaten honeycomb still in her hand.

Cannoc stared at her. He watched as her free hand reached out for something. The goat lowered her head, and Beatryce took hold of her ear.

"So, she is dressed as a monk," said Cannoc. "Her head is shaved. And yet her name is Beatryce."

"Aye," said Jack Dory. "And yet she is Beatryce." He took a bite of the honeycomb. It was sweet and dense.

He looked at Cannoc — his great beard, his unlined face, his huge hands resting loosely upon his knees.

Beatryce trusted him, and as for the

goat, she was not trying to kill the man — which evidenced some degree of trust, he supposed.

Jack Dory said, "She can read. And she can write."

Cannoc nodded.

"The king is looking for her. We are not going toward the king at all, but rather away from him. I believe the king wants to harm her."

"Kings," said Cannoc, "do not know what they want. Except for one thing, of course: they want to keep being kings."

The piece of honeycomb slipped from Beatryce's hand. She kept hold of the goat's ear.

"So," said Cannoc.

"So," said Jack Dory. "The monks of the Order of the Chronicles of Sorrowing shaved her head and dressed her in a monk's robe, but they were afraid to harbor her. They were glad to be rid of her. Except for a wild-eyed monk named Brother Edik. He did not want to send her away. But the head of the order, the man in charge, told me to make sure she did not return to them. Who would think that men of God would be so fear-ful?"

"It could well be that writing the history of the world as those monks do, detailing the terrible things that men do to one another, could make any person afraid," said Cannoc.

Answelica's eyes were closed, but she made a small snort that sounded like agreement.

"Beatryce," said Cannoc very quietly. "Oh, Beatryce."

"Beatryce," agreed Jack Dory. He liked to say her name.

Cannoc leaned forward. He put his face close to Beatryce's.

Answelica opened her eyes and re-garded the man coldly.

"Careful of the goat," said Jack Dory.

"You may be certain of it," said Can-noc. "I have a great deal of respect for the goat."

"Why do you stare at her so?" said Jack Dory.

"Only to learn her face," said Cannoc. "I have looked at many faces in my lifetime, and most I have looked past, never seeing them at all. Now I am attempting to make up for it; I am working to truly see."

There was a bee buzzing around Jack Dory's head. He held out his finger, and the bee hovered near it — humming — and then it flew past him and went to Cannoc and disappeared into the depths of his beard.

Cannoc leaned back. He smiled.

Who was this man that a Granny Bibspeak bee would hide in his beard?

"Who are you?" Jack Dory asked.

"Cannoc, as I said."

"Aye," said Jack Dory. "As you said."

Cannoc nodded. He put his hand to his beard and stroked it.

From somewhere inside his whiskers, the bee hummed.

Chapter Twenty-Nine 🐾

he dreamed.

She dreamed in the warm hollow of a great tree.

She dreamed beside a man with a beard that came down to his knees.

She dreamed before a boy with a sword propped against his leg.

She dreamed leaning against the warmth of a goat.

She dreamed to the sound of a bee buzzing.

What did she dream?

She dreamed of herself.

She watched from a distance.

She watched herself standing in front of the tutor.

She watched herself looking down at the seahorse in the tutor's hand.

"A seahorse," said the tutor. "A horse of the sea."

"Does it live?" Beatryce asked.

"It is dead," said the tutor.

"Make it live again," said Beatryce.

"I cannot do that, Beatryce."

The tutor had dark, curly hair. Balanced atop his head was a circle of daisies. The tutor did not know that the flowers were there.

Beatryce's brothers were off to the side, laughing.

They had put the daisies on the tutor's head. They thought him an overly solemn man, and they felt it would do him good to be made a fool.

Asop and Rowan thought that everyone should be made a bit of a fool.

Asop! Rowan!

Beatryce looked down at herself from the height of the dream. She saw that her hair was long, auburn. The sun shone upon it.

The world was so bright.

164

How could it be that the sun would shine as a nightmare unfolded?

The seahorse was in the tutor's hand, and then it was in Beatryce's hand and she saw it had only the one eye.

Is he made so?

The daisies atop the tutor's head trembled.

Asop and Rowan laughed.

The light shone down.

Rowan's hand jostled the tutor's elbow.

A soldier burst into the room.

The seahorse fell.

Beatryce watched it twist through the air, turning and turning.

It hit the ground and bounced once, twice, three times.

Make it live again!

She watched the great sword of the soldier fly through the air.

Light flashed off the blade of it.

The tutor fell to the ground, and Beatryce went down on her knees beside him.

She screamed once.

Rowan and Asop fell atop her.

Daisies were strewn on the floor. Blood was everywhere. She pretended to be dead.

The sun, unbelievably, continued to shine.

The soldier said, "It is done," and she knew his voice; it was the voice of the man in the dark room at the inn.

Not far from her head was the seahorse. It shone as if it were made of gold.

She heard someone say her name.

Beatryce.

Who was calling her?

Beatryce.

She wanted to answer, but she should not.

Beatryce!

She opened her eyes.

Chapter Thirty

he woke to Jack Dory and Answelica and the man with the beard, Cannoc, staring at her intently.

She woke in the warm heart of a tree with a bee buzzing beside her ear.

"You fell asleep," said Jack Dory.

"You were dreaming," said Cannoc.

The goat, of course, said nothing. But she did what she did best: she looked at Beatryce with conviction and strength and love.

Beatryce started to cry.

"What is it?" said Jack Dory.

But she was crying too much to say what it was. She was weeping an ocean. She would drown in her own tears.

"Can you not say it?" said Jack Dory.

"I remember," said Beatryce.

"What do you remember?" asked Cannoc.

"Who I am."

"Aye," said Jack Dory. He smiled at her. "You are Beatryce."

She cried harder. She nodded.

"What else?" said Cannoc.

"He killed them," said Beatryce. "The soldier came and killed them all. He killed Rowan and Asop. He killed my brothers. He killed the tutor. He intended to kill me. He thought he killed me, but he did not kill me."

A wave of grief crashed over her.

How was it that she was alive and they were dead?

Rowan. Asop. The tutor. The seahorse. The daisies. The light.

It would have been better not to have remembered.

"What of your parents?" said Jack Dory in a quiet voice.

"My father has long been dead," said Beatryce. "He died at war when I was small. I do not remember him."

"And your mother?" asked Cannoc.

Beatryce saw her mother's face — her fierce eyes, her slow smile, the great blazing strength of her.

Oh, her mother!

Beatryce felt as if someone had brought something heavy down upon her head.

"My mother," she said slowly. It was hard, suddenly, to breathe. "My mother was not there. She was not in the room where we were tutored."

"Maybe she lives," said Cannoc.

"Maybe she lives," repeated Beatryce. Her lips felt numb as they repeated the words.

"Aye," said Jack Dory. "Maybe she is even now searching for you."

Beatryce started to cry again.

Cannoc took hold of her hand. Answelica leaned up against her, with her warm, dense, and rough-coated self. Jack Dory took hold of Beatryce's other hand.

The four of them sat together in the tree while Beatryce wept.

In the silence, Beatryce heard her mother's voice: "You must always remember that you are Beatryce of Abelard. Powerful blood runs in your veins."

And then Beatryce remembered the dark room at the inn, the white of the parchment before her, the words written there:

I have killed.

Beatryce looked at Jack Dory. She said, "I am Beatryce of Abelard, and the man who wanted his confession written is the one who killed my brothers. He is the one who killed the tutor and intended to kill me. It was all done at the command of the king."

The bee came again and buzzed at her ear.

"The king," said Beatryce. "The king wants me dead."

Chapter Thirty-One

annoc cleared his throat.

He said, "Perhaps now is the time for me to speak of who I am."

He looked at Jack Dory and then at Beatryce and then at the goat.

He said, "Once, I was king."

Beatryce wiped the tears from her face. She looked up at Cannoc. "You were king?" she said.

"This was long ago. I was king and then I was not. I walked away."

"How does a king walk away?" asked Jack Dory.

"I said to the counselor and to the court, 'I will return momentarily,' and I walked from the throne room. The crown was upon my head. I walked through the great hall, and the servants bowed deeply. I walked out of the castle and to the drawbridge, and the guard there saluted me. I walked across the drawbridge and heard my feet sounding against the wood of it, and I liked the sound of my walking so much that I thought: *I will keep walking.*"

"And you did?" said Beatryce.

"I did," said Cannoc. "I kept walking. I walked into the forest, and the ground beneath my feet felt wondrous — better even than the wood of the drawbridge. I thought: *I will keep walking.*

"I walked unaccompanied. I walked without being accosted. I walked without anyone needing anything of me. It was glorious.

"The birds sang above me. The deer moved past me. I smelled bear and moss and wild honey, and I came to a body of water, a lake I had never seen, and I stood before it and thought of the last words spoken to me. They were from the counselor. His words were 'We shall await your return, sire.'

"I stood for a long time at the lake and

considered those words, and then I took the crown from my head and threw it in the water and watched it disappear. I felt, then, as light as air. I had the thought that without the crown upon my head, I would not be able to keep my feet on the ground."

"The king who could not keep his feet upon the ground," said Beatryce. "It sounds like a story someone would tell."

"Yes, yes," said Cannoc. "It sounds like a story, but it is the truth. I sat down on the ground and laughed and laughed. And, oh, it felt wondrous to laugh. I could not remember the last time I had laughed. I took off my shoes and threw them in the lake along with the crown. And then I put my feet in the water and moved them about and laughed some more, and I thought: *I will never return. I will laugh as often as possible. I will grow my beard. That will be my purpose on this earth: to laugh and to grow my beard and to never, ever return to being a king.*"

"Did they not come looking for you?" asked Jack Dory.

"Come looking for me?" said Cannoc. He laughed. "My child, please understand. No one comes looking for a king. For as soon as a king disappears, those who would replace him start to scheme and calculate about how to take the crown for themselves. Who knows how many kings there have been since I sat upon the throne? Who knows how many schemers and liars have worn a crown? No. No one searches for a missing king."

There was a long silence.

And then Cannoc cleared his throat and said, "That sword." He pointed at the sword leaning against Jack Dory's leg. "That sword bears the mark of the king I once was and am no more. I suppose it has been handed down from a soldier father to a soldier son."

Jack Dory studied the hilt of the sword. He looked at the design embedded in it. "This?" he said, tracing the line with his finger. "What does it mean?"

Beatryce leaned forward. "It is an *E*," she said. "It is the letter *E*."

"I do not know it," said Jack Dory.

"How can you not?" said Beatryce.

"Asop is half your age, and he can read whatever you put before him."

"Perhaps you do not remember, Beatryce," said Cannoc. "Or maybe you never knew. The people cannot read. Only men of God can read, and the king. And tutors and counselors. The people do not know their letters."

Beatryce shook her head. "I remember only that my mother insisted we learn

and that we keep the learning a secret. It is not right that the people cannot read. It is not right at all. I will teach you, Jack Dory. I will teach you to read."

Jack Dory felt something small and glowing inside of him — to read, what would that be like?

He looked at the sword, at the letter upon it, and then he held the sword before him, up high.

"Put it down," said Beatryce, her voice suddenly hollow and cold. "Put it down."

She stood. Answelica stood, too. "I will not be near that sword. I will not have it near me."

Jack Dory laid the sword at his feet. "What would you have me do, Beatryce?" he said. "How should I rid myself of it?"

She stood trembling before him, and he understood her trembling. He knew what it was to watch someone you love die. The robber's dark-bearded face flashed through his mind. He saw, again, the knife clenched between the man's teeth.

The goat lowered her head. She made a low noise of despair.

The bee flew back and forth, back and

forth, between Beatryce and Jack Dory and Cannoc, as if it were tracing some invisible line.

At last, Cannoc spoke. He said, "It could very well be that the sword belongs with the crown."

"Do you mean that we should throw it in the lake?" said Jack Dory.

"No," said Beatryce. Her voice was fierce, certain. "No. I know what must be done. The sword belonged to the soldier; the soldier belonged to the king. The soldier was told to use the sword against me. We will take the sword to the king. We will return his dark deed to him."

"We will?" said Jack Dory.

"Yes," said Beatryce. She stood up very straight. "The king does not need to send his soldiers in search of me."

Answelica looked up at her.

Cannoc, too, stared at Beatryce, but Beatryce kept her eyes on Jack Dory.

"I will tell you what will happen with this sword," she said. "I, Beatryce of Abelard, will hand it to the king. I will make him account for what he has done."

In the dungeon of the king's castle, the counselor stood holding a candle. His robes were as dark as the dungeon itself.

The counselor spoke into the darkness. He said, "You will perhaps be happy to know that the king has made up his mind that Beatryce should live. We are searching for her, Aslyn. And when we find her, I will let the king have his way. At least for a while."

There was a muffled sound of rage.

The counselor waited a long time before he spoke again.

"It may interest you to know that in my role as counselor, in my search for wisdom to lead the king, I did read in the Chronicles of Sorrowing a prophecy that may concern your Beatryce. Would you like to hear this prophecy?"

Silence.

"Very well. It goes like this: 'There will one day come a girl child who will unseat a king and bring about a great change.' I read those words and I thought, *I have* made good use of one prophecy. Why not bend another to my ends?"

He laughed a small laugh.

"Only in this case, I will not make the prophecy come true. No, rather with this overlooked girl-child prophecy, I think I will assure that it does *not* happen as it is written."

There came a strangled cry.

"I am not of noble birth, Aslyn of Abelard, as you once pointed out to me. But it does not matter, does it? I rule in any case. I rule the king. And he who rules the king rules the world."

BOOK
THE
FOURTH

Chapter Thirty-Two

Brother Edik was lost.

Of course he was lost!

How could he be anything but lost?

He, who had set out to find someone with nothing as guidance but the smallest gesture — the innkeeper's wife pointing reluctantly, grudgingly, in the direction of the dark woods.

He, who had always felt so lost in the world in any case.

And the dark woods were so dark!

Always, always, Brother Edik had loathed the dark. He could see things hiding in it — contorted shapes, malignant beings.

His father had known how he feared it.

He had said to Brother Edik's mother, "The boy must learn not to fear so much. Do not take him a light. Do not ever bring him a light when he calls for it. Let him scream. He will get over it soon enough."

But he did not get over it. And every illumination that Brother Edik painted in the Chronicles of Sorrowing — every rising sun or light-dappled tree or shining letter — was in celebration of the beauty of the world and also in defiance of the darkness that had so terrified him as a boy, and terrified him still.

Brother Edik stumbled on a tree root. He righted himself and stumbled again.

He could hear his father laughing. He could hear him saying, "Who are you to think that you could rescue someone? And why, in any case, are you attempting to find the girl? Because of some prophecy that has issued from your own strange head?"

"No," said Brother Edik aloud. "Because she is Beatryce."

Beatryce.

Beatryce, who had looked up at him

and promised that she would write the story of his mermaid.

He must find her.

He had to go forward. He could not, in any case, go back. He could not return to the monastery. He would never again be welcomed there.

There was, truly, no place for him. The home of his childhood was long gone, and it had never been his home, even when he was a child.

His mother had often said to him, "Do not anger your father. Try to do as he says. Try to be who he wants you to be."

But he had not known how to do that, had he?

He still did not know how to do that.

He knew, only, how to be himself.

And shouldn't home be the place where you are allowed to be yourself, loved as yourself?

These were the thoughts swirling through Brother Edik's head when a man suddenly appeared on the path before him.

It is wrong, of course, to say that there was a path.

The dark woods were pathless.

They would not hold a path.

Suffice it to say that suddenly, in the dark woods, there was a man in front of Brother Edik.

The man had a beard. There was a knife clenched in his teeth.

Oh, Beatryce, thought Brother Edik, *I tried. I did try.*

Chapter Thirty-Three

n Cannoc's tree, Beatryce was listening to Jack Dory tell her why it was that she could not go to see the king.

"You will end up dead," said Jack Dory.

"It is foolhardy," said Jack Dory.

"It is idiotic," said Jack Dory.

Cannoc, though, was silent. He sat with his head lowered and his hands resting on his knees.

"You must tell her not to go, Cannoc," said Jack Dory.

Cannoc raised his head and looked at Beatryce. "You said that you are an Abelard."

Beatryce nodded.

"That is an old and noble family," said Cannoc, "a family with much history."

"Well, then," said Beatryce, "who better than me to bring the king to account?"

Jack Dory let out a hiss of exasperation.

"She has a will that can be dangerous," a tutor had once said to her mother.

"Yes," her mother had said in return.

"Should I rein it in, then?" asked the tutor.

He was the first tutor, an oily man whose every word seemed laced with menace.

"You should not," said Beatryce's mother. "She will need it."

"It is a dangerous thing for a girl child to be so set on having her own way," said the tutor.

"Let her have her dangerous will," said her mother.

That tutor had, in the end, left Castle Abelard. He had been dismissed by her mother.

And then, after much time, came the second tutor — the one with the curls. He had with him a bag of wonders. Each day, he took something from it. The final thing he had removed from the bag was the seahorse.

That tutor — the second one, the last one, the good one — had said to her mother, "Beatryce is in possession of a beautiful and agile mind. There is nothing she is not curious about, nothing that she cannot learn."

Her mother nodded. She smiled a small smile. She said, "Teach her everything you can. Let her be as powerful as she can be. Let her be true to what runs in her blood."

"Beatryce?" said Jack Dory now.

"Leave her be," said Cannoc.

Beatryce looked into the goat's eyes. The goat stared back.

Answelica's eyes glowed like strange, shadowed planets.

Beatryce knew of planets.

The last tutor had a special glass that he used to stare up at the stars.

And one early morning, when it was still dark, Beatryce had stood in a field, the tutor beside her and the special glass in her hand. The dew made the hem of her gown heavy. Her feet were cold. She had held the glass up to her eye as the tutor instructed her to do and had seen a glowing orange ball floating in the sky.

"What is it?" she asked the tutor.

"That is something that most people do not even know exists. It is called a planet. It is another world, far from us."

Beatryce had stood looking — her shoes wet, the weight of her dew-dampened gown pulling her to earth, the magic glass to her eye, the tutor breathing beside her — and it was as if someone had pushed aside a dark, heavy curtain and revealed to her a dazzling thing.

She had understood then that the world — and the space beyond it — was filled with marvel upon marvel, too many marvels to ever count.

Beatryce, remembering, shook her head. She took hold of the goat's ear.

She looked at Jack Dory and said, "I will see the king. I will hand him the sword. No one will stop me."

The bee buzzed in circles around Jack Dory's head. Jack Dory looked at her without looking away.

Here was this boy — alive and staring at her.

Rowan was dead. Asop was dead. The tutor was dead.

Beatryce's mother was she did not know where.

But this boy was alive, sitting before her, and he did not know the letter *E*.

"These planets, these other worlds," said the tutor to her that early morning when she looked through the magic glass, "must surely have inhabitants with stories of their own. It is only through ignorance that we do not find our way to them."

Beatryce looked down at her hands, at the dark spots on her thumb and forefinger, the ink.

What world is this I now inhabit, and how shall I live in it?

She looked back up into Jack Dory's waiting face.

She said, "I will go and speak to the king. I will find my mother. No one will stop me. But first, I will teach Jack Dory his letters. I will teach him to read."

Chapter Thirty-Four

ach letter has a shape," Beatryce said. "And each letter has a sound. And you put these shapes and sounds together, and they become words. Do you understand?"

"Aye," he said to her. His heart was beating fast. He did not know — he had not understood — how much he wanted it, to know this secret of letters and sounds and words.

But his heart, pounding against his rib cage, was telling him.

He and Beatryce were bent together over a piece of parchment. Answelica was leaning over them, staring down at the parchment, too.

She gave off a tremendous smell of goat.

192

"You," said Jack Dory, "are in my way." He gave Answelica a small shove.

She butted her forehead against his, shoving him back.

Cannoc was gone. Where he had gone, they did not know. He was off on whatever mysterious errand a man who had once been king and was king no more might need to attend to.

"It begins with this," said Beatryce. "This is the letter *A*, and it is the first one."

She formed the letter.

"*A*," he repeated. He smiled.

"There are twenty-six letters in all," she said. "You will learn each of them, and once you know them, you can mix them as you will, and then use them to form the words of the world and the things of the world. You can write of everything — what is and what was and what might yet be."

Jack Dory nodded.

The inside of Cannoc's tree was snug. There was the smell of beeswax burning, and also, of course, the smell of goat. The bee buzzed around Jack Dory's head

— Granny Bibspeak, beside him, saying, "Learn it, my beloved; learn it all, light of my heart, river of my soul."

"*A* is for *Abelard*. That is my family name. *A* is also the letter that begins the name *Answelica*."

The goat let out an approving grunt.

"The next of the twenty-six is *B*." She bent her head and formed the letter. "*B* is the first letter of my name: *Beatryce*. And from there to *C*."

"What word begins with *C*?" asked Jack Dory.

"Cannoc," said Beatryce.

"And when will we get to the Jack Dory letters?"

"Soon," said Beatryce.

He watched the letters appear one by one beneath her hand, and he felt as if each letter were a door pushed open inside of him, a door that led to a lighted room.

"The world," said Beatryce to Jack Dory, "can be spelled."

Chapter Thirty-Five ❧

he dreamed of standing on a cliff.

Answelica was beside her. They were looking out to sea.

The wind tasted of salt; it blew Beatryce's hair around her face.

She had her hand on Answelica's head.

The sea was green and then blue, and then a deeper blue and then green again.

She heard someone call her name.

She turned. Jack Dory was coming toward her. She smiled at him, and then she looked back at the sea.

And now Jack Dory was beside her, next to her. His shoulder brushed up against her.

"There are seahorses in the sea," said Beatryce.

"Seahorses?" said Jack Dory.

"Yes," said Beatryce, "horses of the sea."

And with those words, the wind blew harder, meaner. The sea went from green to black, and then it tilted and became a dark hallway, and Beatryce was running down the hallway — running away and also running toward.

Where was she going?

She was running to the tower room. She was looking for her mother.

"Mother!" she shouted. "Mother, please!"

She was in Castle Abelard, and she was running down the hallway. But the hallway was so long — longer than it had ever been before. There was no end to it.

She ran and ran, and then, suddenly, she was in the tower room, but her mother was not there.

A blackbird sat in the window. He blinked his dark eyes and opened his black beak and said, "He has taken her."

Beatryce fell to her knees.

"Who?" she said to the bird. "Where?"

A cold wind blew through the room, and the blackbird was gone, and there was nothing anywhere. The entire world was empty.

"Please," she cried.

And then she was awake, and Jack Dory was staring at her.

"You fell asleep again," he said, "sitting up."

Beatryce shook her head. She felt the dream inside of her: the terrible emptiness of the tower room, the wind that blew through it, the blackbird turning to look at her with his dark eyes.

He has taken her.

Where was her mother?

Answelica pushed Jack Dory aside. She offered Beatryce her ear, and Beatryce took hold of it.

"I want my mother," said Beatryce.

"Shhh, now," said Jack Dory. "Tell me your name."

"I am Beatryce of Abelard." The words felt heavy in her mouth.

"Tell me again," said Jack Dory.

"Beatryce of Abelard. I am Beatryce of Abelard."

"Aye," said Jack Dory. He took hold of her hand. "You are Beatryce of Abelard."

"I want my mother. I want Brother Edik. Where is he?"

"I do not know," said Jack Dory.

Beatryce felt, again, the wind from the dream — a cold wind blowing through an empty room.

"There are too many people to miss," she said.

Jack Dory nodded. "Aye," he said. "There are."

He kept hold of her hand, and Beatryce kept hold of Answelica's ear, and they sat so for a long time.

Chapter Thirty-Six

nd where was Brother Edik?

Just where we left him — in the pathless woods, face-to-face with a black-bearded robber.

And what was Brother Edik doing?

He was remembering the words of his prophecy.

There will one day come a girl child who will unseat a king and bring about a great change.

The words appeared before him; they illuminated the darkness around him.

Brother Edik was certain that he was now going to die.

But he was not afraid!

He, who was afraid of everything, was not afraid.

"Can you see me now, Father?" he said aloud. "I am, at last, not afraid!"

He laughed.

The bearded man took the knife from between his teeth. "Funny, is it?"

"It is," said Brother Edik.

"Stop your eye from rolling about like that," said the robber.

"I cannot," said Brother Edik. He laughed again.

"Kneel," said the robber.

Brother Edik went down on his knees. He closed his eyes and saw the mermaid brush, the mermaid's jewel-strewn hair. He saw, for some reason, his father's hand — heavy and battle-scarred. He saw a field of elderhist flowers, bright and glowing.

And then there appeared in his mind the illuminated letter *B*.

B for *Beatryce*.

He saw her face.

Beatryce, who wanted to write the mermaid's story.

Beatryce, who would unseat the king.

And then an image of Answelica appeared before him.

That terrible, wonderful goat.

Her ears were glowing. She looked beautiful to him.

Everything looked beautiful — the mermaid brush, his father's hands, the flowering elderhist, the letter *B,* Beatryce, the goat.

Everything he saw was outlined in gold, illuminated as if he himself had painted it for the Chronicles of Sorrowing.

"Stop smiling," said the robber.

Brother Edik nodded. Yes, yes. He must stop smiling.

The words of the prophecy scrolled through his mind.

There will one day.

There will one day come a girl child.

There will one day come a girl child who will unseat a king.

There will one day come a girl child who will unseat a king and bring about a great change.

He was glad that those words had come to him.

He was glad that Beatryce had come to him, and that he had saved her.

Well, that he and the goat had saved her.

He was glad to have been a part of the story.

Was that enough?

That would have to be enough.

He opened his eyes and saw, in the gloom, the robber's knife above his head.

"Close 'em," said the robber. "I cannot stand how that one eye rolls about."

Brother Edik smiled. He closed his eyes.

And then there came laughter.

Brother Edik wondered if he himself was laughing.

Had he gone mad?

Well, his father would not be surprised.

He held his hand up to his mouth and touched his lips. His mouth was closed: it was not him laughing. But somewhere in the dark woods, there was laughter. It echoed. It went on and on. It seemed to fill the world.

Brother Edik held still. He kept his eyes

closed. He felt the outline of Answelica's hoof on his chest. It burned slightly.

Oh, that goat. He would miss her.

"Take care of her," Brother Edik whispered to the goat. "Guard her."

Suddenly, the laughter ended and the only noise was the rustling of the leaves on the trees.

Brother Edik stayed on his knees, his eyes still closed.

Perhaps he was dead, and he did not yet know it?

There came a hand on Brother Edik's shoulder — warm, solid.

"You are a monk of the Order of the Chronicles of Sorrowing, are you not?" said a voice. "I believe that we have mutual friends."

Brother Edik opened his eyes.

It was so dark! But Brother Edik could see that the black-bearded robber was gone, and that in his place stood a man with a long gray beard.

This man was smiling.

"Come with me," said the man. He held out his hand. And then he laughed and said, "Oh, won't you come a-gallivanting with me?"

Brother Edik took hold of the hand and rose to his feet — alive.

Chapter Thirty-Seven

eatryce was sitting with Jack Dory, showing him his letters, when Answelica stood suddenly, knocking the quill from her hand.

"It is only Cannoc returning," Jack Dory said to the goat.

Cannoc hunched over and entered the tree through the small door, his long beard preceding his body.

"Someone is with him," Jack Dory whispered.

And then Cannoc was standing before them, and behind him was Brother Edik. The monk stood smiling at them, his wild eye dancing in his head.

"Beatryce," he said.

She flung herself into his arms. He

smelled of wool and ink and something sweet — maple.

"Beatryce," he said. "I've been looking for you."

She held him as tight as she was able. Her brothers were dead. Her mother was missing. She had lost everything from her life before. But here, unbelievably, was Brother Edik — who loved her, whom she loved. She held on to him while Answelica did a stiff-legged dance of joy around the two of them.

Cannoc said, "Brother Edik had been detained by one of the robbers of the woods. I came upon him just in time, and we soon sorted everything out. Nothing is more terrifying to evil than joy."

"Brother Edik," said Beatryce. She pulled away from him. She took hold of his hand. She looked into his eyes — the one that was solemn and waiting, the other dancing and rolling in his head. "Much has happened. I have remembered. I know who I am."

She took a deep breath. She did not take her eyes from his.

"I am Beatryce of Abelard, and the

king has ordered me killed. He killed my brothers and my tutor. I do not know where my mother is, or even if she lives."

Brother Edik squeezed her hand, and she drew herself up very straight. "I intend to stand face-to-face with the king. I will have him tell me where my mother is. I will call him to account."

Jack Dory cleared his throat. "But first," he said, "before she goes, Beatryce has agreed to teach me to read and write."

Brother Edik said, "Oh, Beatryce."

"I am teaching him even now," she said.

Brother Edik nodded. He said, "There is a prophecy that is written in the Chronicles of Sorrowing." He spoke very slowly, very carefully. "And this prophecy says that there will one day come a girl child who will unseat a king and bring about a great change."

Beatryce felt the wind from her dream — cold, powerful — blow through her.

"Much has happened," said Cannoc. "Much has yet to happen. We will sit together. We will discuss it."

Chapter Thirty-Eight

And so they sat, the four of them.

Five, if you counted the goat.

And who would not count the goat?

Beatryce rested her hand on Answelica's head; with the other hand, she kept hold of Brother Edik.

They sat in the hollow of the great tree.

They sat gathered around the flame of a candle, and the flame threw their shadows up behind them. There were moments when their shadows looked bigger, much bigger than they themselves were. And then, too, sometimes their shadows seemed to shrink. Big, small, big, small — their five shadows moved against the trunk of the tree.

Beatryce told Brother Edik all of what she remembered — her brothers and the tutor and the soldier and the seahorse falling to the ground.

"How, then, did you find your way to the monastery?" asked Brother Edik.

She shook her head. "I cannot say. I do not remember."

Brother Edik turned to Jack Dory. He said, "And you, Jack Dory, are being tutored by Beatryce."

"Aye," said Jack Dory. "When she does not fall asleep, I am tutored." He smiled. And then he could not help it; he said aloud the letters of the alphabet, one after the other, in the order that Beatryce had told him. He remembered them exactly.

"He knew nothing, Brother Edik," said Beatryce. "The people do not know how to read or write."

"And what of this prophecy?" said Cannoc. "Shall we now speak of that?"

The shadows on the wall danced.

"Is it about Beatryce? The prophecy?" said Jack Dory. "Does it mean she will rule the land?"

"I don't believe there has ever been a queen," said Brother Edik.

"Perhaps it is time," said Cannoc. "After so many kings."

Beatryce sat with her hand on Answelica's head. She looked impossibly small and also bald — not at all like someone who would unseat a king.

"I do not want to be a queen," said Beatryce. "I want only to find my mother and to look the king in the eye and hear him say what he has done."

Beside Beatryce, Answelica held her head high. Her strange eyes glowed.

"Does this prophecy mention a goat?" said Jack Dory.

"It does not mention a goat," said Brother Edik.

"How can it be a true and accurate prophecy without mentioning the goat?" said Jack Dory.

Cannoc laughed and Brother Edik smiled.

But Beatryce looked at them and said, "The prophecy confirms it. I must go to the king."

Her jaw was knotted. There was a look on her face that Jack Dory had learned to recognize and be wary of.

"Some in the world are certain to have their own way," said Jack Dory under his breath. That is what Granny Bibspeak would have said, had she been there.

"What is that?" said Beatryce. "What did you say?"

"Naught," said Jack Dory.

She glared at him; the goat, of course, glared at him, too. It was terrible and overwhelming to have both their ferocious looks trained upon him at the same time.

"It is only that you promised to teach me to read," said Jack Dory.

"And also," said Brother Edik, "you promised me the story of my mermaid."

"Yes," she said. "It is true. I did promise. I promised both of those things."

Chapter Thirty-Nine

t was late at night. They were all asleep in Cannoc's tree.

But Beatryce could not sleep. She could not keep herself from sorting through what she knew and did not know, what she had dreamed and what she remembered.

For instance: she had not told the others that she remembered standing up.

Once it was silent, once the only sound in the world was the beating of her own heart, she had stood up and walked away from her brothers and the tutor.

Who would want to admit to such a thing — to walking away from people you loved?

But she had done it. She had stood up

and walked away.

Nor did she tell them what she had dreamed — the cliff and the sea and her hair long, and the wind in her face and Answelica beside her and Jack Dory coming toward her — a dream of the future, she was sure of it.

If the prophecy was about her, she must face it.

She did not want to be queen, but still she had to go to the king.

She had to find her mother.

And yet she had promised Brother Edik that she would write the story of his mermaid.

And there was Jack Dory to consider — his face open, alight, as she told him each of the letters and how they could be combined to name the world.

She had promised him, too.

She put out her hand and touched Answelica's bony, warm head.

The goat's eyes opened and looked into hers. Planets. Other worlds.

Beatryce remembered again standing in the morning darkness with the tutor, holding the magic glass and staring up at the glowing planet.

"Do you think that the people on this other world are standing and looking through a magic glass at us?" she said to the tutor. "Could it be that they are wondering about us even as we are wondering about them?"

The tutor put a hand on her shoulder.

"Beatryce," he said.

"Yes."

"Your father was a great friend of mine. He believed very much in knowledge and learning."

She did not look away from the planet. She kept the glass pointing at the sky. She could feel her hand tremble. "I did not know him," she said. "He died and I have no memory of him."

"He wanted you to know as much as could be known," said the tutor. "It is your birthright. That is what he believed."

"I want to learn."

"I will teach you everything I can, everything I am able, so that if a different day comes, you will be ready."

But he hadn't taught her everything he could.

He had been killed before he could do that.

The king had ordered him killed.

And the day had come, hadn't it? The different day had come.

She must be ready now.

There was, in truth, no time to waste.

She could not keep the promises she had made. At least she could not keep them now.

She stood and, in the darkness of Cannoc's tree, the goat stood, too.

"Shhh," said Beatryce. "Come."

Together, she and the goat stepped around the sleeping forms of Cannoc and Brother Edik and Jack Dory. They went through the small door into the great darkness outside.

Beatryce stood for a moment and looked up. She saw the stars, hundreds of them, thousands of them, and she thought she saw a planet — surely, there was a planet up there, too — looking down at her.

And then, without warning, the stars

disappeared, and the world became nothing but darkness. There was an overwhelming smell of mold and blood.

"Don't make a sound," said a voice. She was pulled tighter into the darkness.

Did she call out?

She did not.

She knew what had happened.

She knew who had come for her.

Chapter Forty 🙎🙐

he goat stood over Jack Dory.

Her breath was hot on his face.

She said nothing. She was capable of saying nothing.

She was only a goat.

But he woke to her bright eyes staring at him, and it was as good as if she had spoken.

"Now is the time for that sword, you."

Jack Dory reached for the sword. He wrapped his hand around the hilt and leapt to his feet.

He stood, breathing hard, holding the sword in front of him. He looked around in the darkness. Brother Edik. Cannoc. Answelica.

But there was no Beatryce. His heart was beating fast, slamming against the walls of his chest.

"Beatryce!" he shouted.

The goat butted her head against his legs, pushing him forward.

He bent and went through the door and out into the world, where the stars were shining magnificently, indifferently.

"Beatryce!" Jack Dory shouted again.

He heard rustling, the sound of branches breaking.

The goat butted her head into his right leg. She looked up at him with desperate eyes. Answelica knew what had happened, but she could not say it.

Brother Edik came out of the door in the tree. Behind him was Cannoc.

The two men were nothing but shadows in the darkness under the bright stars. They were all nothing but shadows.

"She's gone," said Jack Dory. He thought he might cry. The sword felt cold in his hands, worthless.

Cannoc put his hand on Jack Dory's shoulder.

"We will find her," he said.

"We three will go and find her," said Brother Edik.

Answelica made a small strangled noise.

"We four," said Cannoc. "We four will find her."

Jack Dory stood holding the sword. It was a heavy thing. His heart was heavy, too. It was, he reckoned, a heart full of too many things. It carried the letters of the alphabet, waiting to be fashioned into words. It carried Granny Bibspeak, and his parents, and Beatryce.

How much could a heart hold?

The bee buzzed above his head.

He looked down at Answelica. Her eyes spoke to him. They said, "Now. Hurry. There is no time to waste. We must go to the castle of the king."

The goat.

The goat was in his heart, too. Seemingly, the heart could hold an untold amount of things — letters and people and goats and bees.

Seemingly, there was no limit to what it could contain.

Jack Dory lifted the sword.

The blade of it gleamed in the light of the indifferent stars.

"We must go now," Jack Dory said to the others.

And then he repeated what the goat had told him, what he knew to be true: "There is no time to waste. We must go to the castle of the king."

Chapter Forty-One

he was on the back of a horse, wrapped tightly in a scratchy and terrible-smelling cloth — a blanket or cloak.

Whoever had captured her did not talk. There was breathing. The sound of a horse's hooves. The clink of spurs. But there were no words, and Beatryce thought that this was the fourth darkness.

The first darkness had been when she lay beneath her brothers' bodies.

The second darkness was when she found her way to the monastery and woke in the barn, holding Answelica's ear, remembering nothing that had come before.

The third darkness was when she sat on

the floor of the room at the inn and heard the confession of the soldier.

Each time, she had found her way out into the light — with the help of a goat, a monk, a boy.

But this time? What of this time?

In his bag of wonders, the tutor had a book. The pages of it were glossy and slick, and they were sewn together in a complicated and elegant way, so that the stitches did not show at all. The words in the book were printed uniformly, evenly, and each page was filled with lavish illustrations.

The book told the story of a wolf who was, in truth, a king.

The king had been cursed by a witch and turned into a wolf, and he went through the world with the crown upon his head, buried beneath his thick wolf fur. No one could see the crown; thus, no one believed that he was the king.

In the book, there was a picture of the night sky, blue unto black, and in the sky, there was a moon on its side, looking down at the wolf with sadness and wonder.

The moon, alone, knew who the wolf truly was.

Until a small girl came along.

The girl could see the glint of the crown beneath the fur.

She said to the wolf, "I see your crown."

And with these words, the wolf partially transformed before her. He became, then, half king and half wolf.

The more the girl believed in the king in him, the more the king appeared.

But if she stopped believing, the king would disappear, and there was nothing then but wolf — sharp-clawed and long-toothed — enraged at not being seen for who he truly was.

The girl said to him, "I am tired of believing you into existence. It is too much work. You must believe for yourself that you are king."

The girl went away after she spoke these words, and the wolf sat alone under the blue-black sky with the moon looking down on him — studying him, pitying him.

But slowly, slowly, the wolf believed him-

self into the king he was. He transformed the whole of himself with the exception of his left paw. That — the paw — he could not seem to undo, to make human again. The magic that the witch had put in place there could not be unwoven. But as for the rest of him: he was king and not wolf, and that is how he stayed.

After a long time, the girl returned to him. She was a grown woman, and she said to him, "You believed for yourself who you are."

The king replied, "I did."

And they were then king and queen together. They ruled side by side.

It was only they two who knew that one of the king's hands was, in truth, the paw of something wild.

They knew and the moon knew.

And the reader of the story knew, too.

The book ended with words spoken by the wise queen. Those words were: "We shall all, in the end, be led to where we belong. We shall all, in the end, find our way home."

On the back of the horse, wrapped in the foul cloth, Beatryce remembered the words at the end of the book, remembered, too, writing them down before the monks at the monastery.

Even when she had been able to recall nothing at all about who she was, she had remembered the words of this story.

Why?

Perhaps because she had loved the book so much — the feel of its pages in her hand, its deep-hued illustrations, its uniformly printed words.

When she was done reading the book, Beatryce had told the tutor that she wanted another one like it — another book that was full of transformations and discoveries, wolves and moons, curses and becomings.

The tutor had said, "There are no other books that tell stories, Beatryce. This is the only one I know of and have ever seen."

"Why are there no such books?" she asked him.

"They are not allowed."

"Why are they not allowed?"

"There are many things that are not

allowed, Beatryce," he said. "That is a discussion for another time."

She thought, now, about the wolf.

She thought about the moon in the sky that watched the wolf and waited for him to believe in who he was. Were the stars watching her? And the planets? Were they waiting for her to believe in who she was?

And who was she, in any case?

Not a queen. That much she knew. It was not her destiny to rule.

What, then, was her destiny?

Beatryce thought of the girl who saw the wolf for who he was.

She thought about the wonder of being known by others for who you were — beloved.

She wanted, suddenly, to say to this person who had taken her, who had wrapped her in a stinking cloth and put her on the back of a horse, that she was beloved. And that those who loved her — a wild-eyed monk, a man who had once been king, a boy who knew his letters, a goat with a head as hard as stone — would come searching for her.

Thinking of Answelica's head and the damage it was capable of inflicting cheered Beatryce considerably.

The goat was capable of anything.

The goat would find her somehow.

They would all find her — Brother Edik and Jack Dory and Cannoc.

What is it to know that people will come searching for you?

Everything.

We shall all, in the end, be led to where we belong.

We shall all, in the end, find our way home.

Chapter Forty-Two

he was right.

They came looking for her.

They left at dawn, Jack Dory holding the sword.

He had wanted to leave in the middle of the night, but Cannoc had said to him, "If you are going to carry that thing with you, then you must have the knowledge of how to use it."

"Aye," said Jack Dory. "And who will teach me?"

"I will," said Cannoc, "this very night. I was once a warrior and carried a sword. I have put down my arms and armor, but I can instruct you."

It would be good if it could be said that Jack Dory struggled to learn what Cannoc taught him.

Alas, that is not the case at all.

Jack Dory did not struggle.

Swordplay came as easily to him as everything else did.

Cannoc showed him and he learned, and the sword, with its terrible history, was not heavy in Jack Dory's hands. He found that if he moved it just as Cannoc said he must — fast and furious and certain and without regret — the sword made a high whistling as it went through the air, almost as if it were singing.

Jack Dory, the sword in his hands, thought that he would like, now, to come upon that black-bearded robber who had killed his parents.

He thought, too, that he would like to meet whoever had taken Beatryce.

Yes, Jack Dory and his sword would like to meet them all.

BOOK
THE
FOURTH

Chapter Forty-Three

hat does it mean to be brave?

This was a question that Brother Edik asked himself as he walked through the dark woods with Jack Dory and Cannoc and Answelica.

To be brave is to not turn away.

To be brave is to go forward.

To be brave is to love.

Brother Edik was not turning away. He was going forward.

And he loved. This, Brother Edik could do — did do — best of all.

Still, he could not keep himself from trembling.

And he could not stop the words of

the prophecy from tumbling through his mind:

A girl child

unseat a king

great change.

It was, to him, deeply unsettling and deeply moving to find that these words of his were true.

Cannoc walked beside Brother Edik; ahead of them was Jack Dory — the sword in his hands and the goat beside him. Brother Edik thought it was possible that Answelica was even more dangerous than the sword.

It was a comfort to have her walking out front.

If you had told Brother Edik a short time ago that he would be walking through the woods behind a demon goat, that he would be following a boy with a sword, that he would be walking beside a man who had once been king, Brother Edik would have believed none of it.

Where, Brother Edik wondered, *was the prophecy for all of this?*

He put his hands in the pocket of his

robe and found the maple candies. He had forgotten to give them to Beatryce. He took hold of a candy in the shape of a leaf and thought, *Beatryce, we are coming for you. I am bringing you something sweet. And you, in turn, must tell me the story of the mermaid. You must teach Jack Dory to read.*

You promised, Beatryce.

And I promise: we are coming for you.

He sent this message to her over the trees of the dark woods, across the fields blooming with elderhist, and up to the lightening sky. He sent the message all the way to the castle of the king.

Beatryce, we are coming for you.

Chapter Forty-Four

he was in a cell in a dungeon.

She was no longer wrapped in the cloak, but she might as well have been; it was that dark in the cell.

Her head itched. Before they had all gone to sleep in Cannoc's tree, Brother Edik had told her that this was because her hair was growing back. Were those the last words Brother Edik had spoken to her? And if so, why could they not have been more important words?

She remembered, suddenly, being in the tower room.

Her mother was at the spinning wheel, and Beatryce was at her feet, bent over the tutor's book about the king who had been turned into a wolf. She was reading the story to her mother, and her mother was nodding, smiling, spinning.

The small room was filled with light.

"It is very good, Beatryce," said her mother. "It is a good story, and you read it wonderfully well. But remember, if someone outside of this house were ever to ask you if you could read or write, you must say that you cannot. You must never admit to what you can do. There may well come a day when things will be different and you can claim your powers. But for now we must be careful. Do you understand?"

"Yes," Beatryce had said.

Although she had not, truly, understood.

But her mother had understood. Her mother had known.

Her mother.

Where was she?

The dream of the long hallway and the empty tower room and the blackbird sitting in the window blew through her.

He has taken her.

"Do not think of it," she said aloud to herself.

What, then, to think of?

Answelica. Her head like a rock. Her eyes like planets. Her great and ferocious love.

Surely, the goat was on her way. Surely, they were all on their way to her.

Beatryce wrapped her arms around her legs to warm herself. It was cold, very cold.

She felt as though the darkness were trying to swallow her up.

She must not allow that to happen. She must stay herself.

"You promised me the story of my mermaid," Brother Edik had said to her.

"Very well, Brother Edik," she said aloud. "I will tell you the story of the mermaid."

And so she went back to the words she had written in that other darkness — the darkness of the soldier's room at the inn.

Once, there was a mermaid.

"Once, there was a mermaid."

Those were the words that Beatryce of

Abelard said to herself in the dungeon, in the castle of the king.

She let the words of the story rise up as if they were already written on the pages of a book. She made believe that she was reading the words aloud, telling a story to someone she loved in a room filled with light.

Once, there was a mermaid.

Chapter Forty-Five 🙖🙔

t was late morning when they came upon the black-bearded robber.

He dropped from a tree in front of Jack Dory. The knife was between his teeth.

He said, "I'll take that pretty sword."

But the words were hardly out of his mouth before Answelica lowered her head and sent the robber flying through the air with such force that the knife fell from his mouth and went flying, too.

When the robber landed, the goat stood over him. She showed him her terrible teeth. She bit him in the arm. And then she danced from hoof to hoof, waiting for the man to stand up so that she could send him flying again.

Jack Dory would have laughed at it all, but there was nothing to laugh about.

He knew this man.

This was the one who had killed his parents. How often had he dreamed of that black beard and bright knife? How many times had he longed to be face-to-face with the man and exact his revenge?

Jack Dory went and stood beside the dancing goat. He put the tip of his sword at the man's throat.

"Do not," came Cannoc's voice.

"This one," said Jack Dory. "He is the one who killed my mother and my father." His voice shook. "I see him every night in my dreams, and now I will kill him and see him no more."

"Killing him will not banish him from your dreams," said Cannoc. "I can assure you of that. Think on who you are, Jack Dory."

"I'm thinking on it," said Jack Dory. "I am well and truly thinking on it."

His heart stuttered. The goat danced. Jack Dory kept the tip of the sword on the man's neck.

Cannoc bent down and picked up the robber's knife. He held it out so that Jack Dory could see it. "Here is the man's knife," said Cannoc. "He is nothing without it."

Jack Dory looked at the knife, and then he looked back again into the robber's face. He pressed the tip of the sword harder against the man's throat.

Answelica made a high, impatient noise. She moved from hoof to hoof. She displayed her terrible teeth.

"Come, come," she seemed to say. "There is no time to waste on revenge. We must find her."

Jack Dory wondered when it was that he had started to hear what the goat was thinking.

It was troublesome, having goat thoughts in his head.

Again, he pressed the sword deeper. The world narrowed to nothing but Jack Dory and the sword and the robber's neck.

"Go on and do it," said the robber through gritted teeth. "I don't care."

Jack Dory looked away from the man.

He bent his head back. Up high in the sky, beyond the trees, beyond the dark woods and the robber and the sword and the goat and the knife, the sun was shining.

Jack Dory kept his sword where it was. He felt the sun warm on his face. The bee buzzed around his head.

If he moved his fingers just so, he could feel the letter engraved upon the hilt of the sword. It was an *E*. He had not known that, and now he did know it.

The letter *E*.

Letters.

Letters that became words. Words that became stories. Stories that told what had happened, what would happen.

The bee buzzed louder.

Bee, which began with the letter *B*. And then what? What letters came next?

"How is it that you spell the word *bee*?" Jack Dory asked, his face still tilted up to the sun.

"What?" said the robber.

"It begins with the letter *B*," said Brother Edik.

"Aye," said Jack Dory. "That I know. And then what?"

"The *B* is followed by an *E* and then another *E*," said Brother Edik. His voice was calm, certain.

"*B-E-E*, is it?" said Jack Dory.

"It is," said Brother Edik.

Answelica made another noise of impatience.

"The letters are put together to form words," said Jack Dory, "and the words name the things of the world."

"Yes," said Brother Edik.

Jack Dory closed his eyes and opened them again. He lowered his head and looked down at the robber.

"You killed my parents," said Jack Dory.

"If you say I did," said the man. He smiled.

"Stand up," said Jack Dory.

The robber rose slowly to his feet. Jack Dory kept his sword at the man's neck all the while.

"You," said Jack Dory, "are nothing. You are only someone who takes."

The robber grinned. "Just as you say.

Wasn't it me who took the soldier to your little friend?"

Beside Jack Dory, the goat tensed up, held still.

"A soldier of the king?" said Jack Dory.

"Who else?" said the robber.

"Forget him, boy," Jack Dory heard Answelica say. "It is as I said. All that matters now is that we find her."

Jack Dory spat at the man's feet. He said, "It makes no difference to me whether you live or die. None at all." He lowered the sword. His arm ached from holding it out before him.

Cannoc handed Jack Dory the robber's knife. "Come," he said.

"Now!" said the goat.

Jack Dory slid the knife into his belt. He turned his back on the robber and walked away.

The boy followed the goat.

Cannoc and Brother Edik followed the boy.

And a bee buzzed happily, approvingly, around Jack Dory's head as he walked forward, away.

Chapter Forty-Six

 man came to Beatryce in the dungeon. He was carrying a candle and dressed in a black cloak. He smelled of cloves and rancid oil.

"I am counselor to the king," he said. "You will stand."

Beatryce slowly stood. She was glad, so glad, to see the candle, to see the little bit of light.

"So," said the counselor. "Here, then, is Beatryce, Beatryce of Abelard."

"Yes," she said.

"The one of whom the prophecies speak."

"Yes," she said again. She stood straighter.

"Proud, are you?" said the counselor. "Prophecies mean nothing, my child. They are nothing but shiny baubles, bright distractions, pretty words used to manipulate kings and comfort fools."

The man's voice was familiar to her. Why?

The counselor held the candle in such a way that it illuminated her face and not his own.

"Who are you?" she said. She wrapped her hands around the bars of the cell. She tried to see the counselor's face.

"Ah. You are remembering, I see. You are recalling. Yes. It will come to you, I'm sure. In the meantime, what if I were to tell you a story?"

She said nothing.

"The story begins this way: Once, there was a learned man, and one fine day, he came to a castle perched on the edge of a sea. The man had been called to the castle to tutor the three children of a nobleman. The nobleman had died fighting in some war, for some cause or another. Who knows what it was.

"So. The learned man came to the

castle to teach this man's children. And you can imagine the man's surprise when he found that the eldest of the three was a girl and that he was expected to tutor her as well.

" 'I cannot teach a girl,' said the learned man. 'It is against the law.'

" 'I wish her to be educated,' said the noblewoman. 'And her father agreed with my wishes.'

"Well, the learned man was so bewitched by the beauty and charms of this woman that he did as she asked. He broke the law. He taught the girl to read and write. She learned very quickly."

"Do not tell me any more," said Beatryce. "I do not want to hear."

"You will listen to what I tell you, Beatryce of Abelard. You will listen to all of it. So. The learned man fell in love with the nobleman's wife. He offered himself to her. But she would not accept his love.

"You see, this woman had a twisted notion in her head that one day her children might rule the kingdom — yes, that even her daughter might be in a position of power. She told the learned man this and he laughed at her. Most likely, she assumed that because he was not of noble birth, he would never understand the duties of lineage and power. She dismissed him. He went away from Castle Abelard."

The counselor now held the candle up close to his face so that she could see it. He smiled.

"Yes," he said. "You know me, Beatryce. You know me well. I am the one who taught you to read. I am the one who was sent away from you. But no matter. It has all turned out quite well. In spite of the fact that I am not of noble birth, I have made my way to the halls of power.

"I am a maker of destinies. I made a king. This king was nobody. Do you know how many youngest sons of youngest sons there are? But I made the prophecy come true. I made him king, and now I control him, which means I control everything. Do you understand?"

She did understand. And she was terrified. But she stood straight and true and said, "I would like to see this king."

The counselor laughed, and the sudden gust of air from his mouth made the candle flame flicker. "You would like to see the king."

"Yes," said Beatryce.

"And what of your mother? Would you like to see her as well?"

Beatryce felt her heart fall to her toes. The long hallway flashed through her mind, and then came the empty tower room and the blackbird turning to look at her and saying, "He has taken her."

"Where is she?" she whispered. "Where is my mother?"

"All in good time, Beatryce. First, I will go and have a word with the king. I will let him know that you have safely arrived. He has been waiting for you."

The counselor blew out the candle, and the darkness returned full force.

"You see how it is," he said. "You see who is in charge here. It is not you. It is no longer you. Or your mother."

Chapter Forty-Seven

*e has taken her.*

"But where?" she said aloud. "Where has he taken her? Where is she?"

Her heart was beating very fast. Was the prophecy true? Was it about her at all? Was it nothing but pretty words?

She could not think about it anymore, any of it, or she would go mad.

Once, there was a mermaid.

The story. That is what she must do. She must write the story. But she could not write it. There was nothing to write with, and it was too dark to write, in any case.

She sat on the floor of the dungeon with her hands in her lap and the dark all around her, and she thought, *I will tell this story nonetheless. No one can stop me from telling this story.*

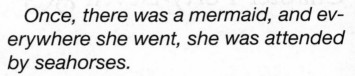

Once, there was a mermaid, and everywhere she went, she was attended by seahorses.

The seahorses combed the mermaid's long hair. They whispered her seahorse stories and sang her seahorse songs in their high-pitched seahorse voices. The stories were strange stories and the songs were strange songs, but they pleased the mermaid. She swam through the sea attended by seahorses and was never alone.

"Do not go too far," said the mermaid's mother. "Listen to the advice of the seahorses. And if you go above water, do not stay there for long."

"Yes," said the mermaid. "I promise."

But sometimes, even though the seahorses advised against it most strenuously, the mermaid went out of the water and sat upon a large rock

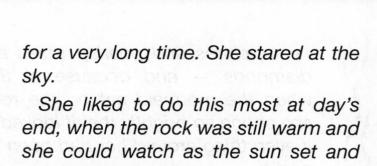

for a very long time. She stared at the sky.

She liked to do this most at day's end, when the rock was still warm and she could watch as the sun set and the stars appeared.

The seahorses stayed in the water. They were not pleased. They swam around the rock, muttering their dark warnings and occasionally breaking into song.

There was one old seahorse who had lost an eye in some long-ago seahorse war. His name was Morelich, and his voice was loudest of all.

"Very wrong," he said. "Most dangerous. Descend, descend. Return to the water. Return."

The mermaid ignored him. She ignored all of them. She looked up at the sky and then down at her tail, which shone magnificently in the light.

Her tail was scaled, of course, as all mermaid tails are.

But this mermaid's tail was also different. It was encrusted with jewels

— sapphires and pearls, rubies and diamonds — and because of this, when the mermaid sat on the rock, she shone so brightly that it looked as if everything around her had been set on fire.

What was the mermaid's name?

Rosellyn.

Her name was Rosellyn.

This was the beginning of the story.

Beatryce said the words aloud until she had them just as she wanted them.

When she fell silent, she heard something scuttling about in the darkness, and something dripping, and sometimes, too, from what seemed like very far away, the sound of weeping, the sound of some great sorrow.

Chapter Forty-Eight

e are close now," said Cannoc.

He fell back and let Answelica and Jack Dory take the lead again.

As they neared the castle, Cannoc changed. His shoulders became rounded, his face more lined. He did not laugh.

"You can turn back," Brother Edik said to him. "We three will go to the king without you."

"No," said Cannoc. "It must be done, and I will do it."

"What happens when a king enters the castle where he once ruled?" asked Brother Edik.

"I do not know," said Cannoc. "There have been many kings since me. Perhaps they will not remember me." He shrugged. And then he sang a small song:

> *"We do not know what*
> *will become.*
> *What will become*
> *is what becomes,*
> *and that is all*
> *we know."*

Cannoc looked over at Brother Edik and smiled.

"But do you believe the prophecies that are written in the Chronicles of Sorrowing?" asked Brother Edik.

"I visited the book when I was king," said Cannoc. "And my counselor went often and studied it, as all counselors must. He told me what it said. And yet."

"And yet?" said Brother Edik.

"And yet there was no prophecy written that said I would walk away from my throne. But I did. I did walk away."

"And what of Beatryce? Do you believe the prophecy about her? That she will unseat the king?"

"What will become is what becomes, and that is all I know," said Cannoc.

Ahead of them, Answelica walked with her head up high, taking in great snorts of air as if she could smell Beatryce nearby.

Cannoc said, "I do believe the best and wisest thing we can do is to follow the goat."

Brother Edik smiled.

They walked in silence then. The dust of the road rose up around them in brown clouds that hovered and fell with their footsteps.

Jack Dory turned and looked at the men.

"Why do you go so slowly when we are so near?" he said.

Answelica turned also. She gave them both a look laced with threats of violence.

"Go on, go on," said Cannoc. "We are following."

The goat and the boy turned and went on.

"I wonder," said Cannoc, "if you believe in the prophecy of Beatryce. Do you want it to be true?"

"I want her to know that we came for

her," said Brother Edik. "That is what I want above all things, for her to know that we came for her."

"Yes," said Cannoc. "Well, then, what you believe in is love."

"I suppose so," said Brother Edik. He put his hands into the pocket of his robe and found a maple candy in the shape of a flower. He pulled it out and held it in the palm of his hand. "Here," he said to Cannoc.

"Ah," said Cannoc. "Something sweet." His face filled with a sudden light. "Is there just the one candy? Or do you have another, so that the boy may have one, too?"

Brother Edik pulled a crescent moon from his pocket.

Cannoc's face became brighter still. "I believe that the goat could benefit from some sweetness, don't you?"

Brother Edik retrieved a maple candy in the shape of a little man.

"Excellent," said Cannoc. "I thank you." He took the candies from Brother Edik. He called out, "Jack Dory! Answelica! Here is something for you!"

He walked toward the boy and the goat, carrying the candy in his outstretched hand. He was smiling.

Chapter Forty-Nine

The story of the mermaid came to her as if she had read it long ago, as if there had been another book in the tutor's bag of wonders and she had read its contents and seen its pictures and remembered the whole of it.

"How does it go, now, Beatryce?" she asked herself. "What happens next? You must remember."

And it so happened that there were sailors who saw the mermaid on the rock one evening.

They saw the sun's rays catching the light of the jewels encrusted in her tail, and the sailors were properly dazzled, and they spoke to one another again and again about what they had seen.

They could not get over it.

They felt that it was a good and wondrous thing — that they had been promised something — each time they caught sight of the mermaid and her jeweled tail.

The sailors' stories of the mermaid were told and retold until they reached the ears of the king, who learned that there was a mermaid whose tail was studded with sapphires and pearls, rubies and diamonds.

The king thought that his life would not be complete until he could own this mermaid and her jeweled tail. And the counselor said to the king, "You must indeed have the mermaid. You must have whatever you want, Your Majesty."

And so the counselor sent the king's soldiers out to find her.

If only Rosellyn had heeded the words of the one-eyed seahorse!

If only she had listened to her mother and had not stayed above the water so long!

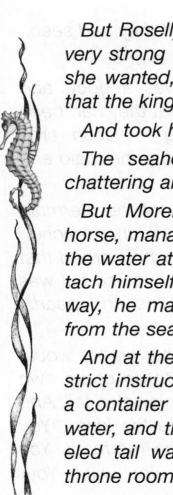

But Rosellyn was a mermaid with a very strong will and she had done as she wanted, and so it came to pass that the king's men found her.

And took her.

The seahorses were left behind, chattering and wailing.

But Morelich, the one-eyed seahorse, managed to fling himself from the water at the last moment and attach himself to Rosellyn's tail. In this way, he made the journey with her from the sea to the castle of the king.

And at the castle of the king, under strict instructions from the counselor, a container was built and filled with water, and the mermaid with the jeweled tail was put on display in the throne room.

"Terribleness," Morelich whispered into her ear. "Do not speak. Do not look. Do not meet their eyes. Never. Never."

The king stared at her, and the noblemen and the noble ladies stared at her. And the king's counselor stared at her, too, and smiled a terrible smile.

264

Rosellyn kept her eyes lowered.

She looked away.

She said nothing.

She grew wan.

She thought often of the words from a story that the seahorses had once told her: What world is this I now inhabit, and how shall I live in it?

And then it happened that her jewels began to fall away.

One by one, the sapphires and pearls and rubies and diamonds turned to ordinary stones that sank to the bottom of the container.

The king ordered the stones collected and broken open, and it was done.

"They are nothing but rocks through and through, sire," said the counselor.

The king was enraged.

He stood before the mermaid and said, "You will turn the rocks back into jewels. I command it!"

But Rosellyn did not know how to do this.

 *Morelich whispered in her ear. He said, "They will destroy you. Do not let them. Do not let them destroy you."*

Beatryce stopped speaking the words of the story.

There was a light coming toward her.

"Who is there?" she called.

She heard again, from far away, the sound of weeping.

The light grew bright.

It was the king, a great golden crown upon his head.

Beatryce stood.

"I wanted to see your face," the king said to Beatryce. "My counselor says that you are the one of whom the prophecy speaks. He says that I should not doubt him. But I wanted to see your face to know if it was true."

He held the candle out before him and studied her.

Beatryce wanted to say to the man, *You killed my brothers. You tried to kill me. But you failed. Here I stand before you. You failed.*

But she did not say it. Instead, Beatryce opened her mouth and said one word: "Once."

Once.

"Yes?" said the king. He leaned toward her.

"Once," said Beatryce of Abelard, "there was a mermaid, and everywhere she went, she was attended by seahorses."

Chapter Fifty

eep within the bowels of the castle, Beatryce told the king a story, and outside the castle, there came a monk and a goat, an old bearded man bent over a cane, and a boy with a sword.

Brother Edik and Cannoc stayed back while Jack Dory and Answelica approached the castle drawbridge. It was guarded by two soldiers.

Jack Dory turned to the goat. He said, "Is she here?"

Answelica put her nose up in the air and sniffed. She looked at Jack Dory from the corner of her eye. She nodded.

This goat! He loved her!

He nodded back. "Well, then, we will go and do what we can do."

Together, he and Answelica approached the guards at the drawbridge.

"I have come to see the king!" said Jack Dory.

The sun was shining brightly. Answelica was giving off a powerful smell of goat. The bee was buzzing in lazy circles around Jack Dory's head, the sword was resting on his shoulder, and there was not a cloud in the sky.

"Ha," said the guard on the left. "The boy has come to see the king."

"Ha-ha," said the guard on the right. "He has come to see the king."

"Brought your goat with you, did you?" said the left guard.

"She is not my goat," said Jack Dory. "She is her own goat, and I must warn you: She is as anxious to see the king as I am. She is very set on getting her way, this goat. And it does not take much to anger her."

Answelica danced from hoof to hoof. Jack Dory put a hand on her head, to stop her from sending the guards flying.

The right guard said, "The goat is anxious to see the king, and it don't take much to anger the goat."

The left guard said, "I heard it, didn't I? It don't take much to anger the goat."

Jack Dory felt Answelica's body quiver with rage. There was not much time.

"I have come to return something to the king," said Jack Dory. "This sword. It did once belong to a king, and I am returning it."

The left guard reached forward and took the sword from Jack Dory's hands. "Now you have returned it. Get along, boy."

And then came Cannoc's voice. He was singing.

> *"I bring,*
> *I bring,*
> *I bring*
> *word.*
> *I bring*
> *word for*
> *the king."*

Cannoc bent low over the cane, tucked his head, and kept his face hidden as he approached the soldiers.

The left guard spat at Cannoc's feet. "Go on, beggar," he said. "The king does not want your words."

But Cannoc continued to sing.

> *"I bring,*
> *I bring*
> *word.*
> *I bring word*
> *and truth.*
> *I bring truth*
> *and sorrowing.*

I bring a prophet
for the king."

He stopped singing and shouted, "Perhaps you have not heard me! I have brought a prophet to the king!"

Brother Edik stepped forward, his eye rolling in his head, his whole being trembling.

He said to the guards, "You will admit the boy, and you will admit the goat. You will admit the beggar. You will admit me! I am the prophet who brings words of warning for the king! Hear my words! You will make a dire mistake if you do not admit us!" His eye rolled wildly in his head.

He looked absolutely, positively mad.

His words were followed by a high noise of keening from Answelica.

Jack Dory knew that the sound the goat made was one of impatience and rage, but to untutored ears, the goat's scream sounded otherworldly, terrifying.

The left guard and right guard looked at each other.

Together, they motioned for the drawbridge to be lowered.

Jack Dory felt a wild shot of joy go through him.

He would enter the castle.

He would find her.

He would see her face again.

The bee buzzed triumphantly around his head.

Bee.

B-E-E.

B.

For *Beatryce.*

Chapter Fifty-One

 In the dungeon, Beatryce told the king a story. "And so it was," said Beatryce. She stood with her forehead pressed against the bars of the cell. The king leaned toward her.

She took a deep breath and said, "And so it was that the noblemen and noble ladies did not come anymore to look at the mermaid and her tail."

The king sighed.

Beatryce continued.

The container with the mermaid in it was moved to a tower room high up in the castle. The mermaid was alone, except for the one-eyed sea-

horse Morelich, who spoke nothing but words of doom.

And then, after a time, even Morelich fell silent.

Rosellyn missed her mother. She missed the great green depths of the sea. She missed the chorus of seahorses whispering seahorse stories and seahorse songs in her ear.

There was a char boy who came once a day to the tower room to feed the mermaid, but Rosellyn turned her back to him and would not let him see her face.

She did not speak to him.

She spoke to no one.

Late in the afternoon, the sun entered the tower room through one narrow window. The mermaid looked at the rays of the sun and thought how she would never again see her mother.

And then one day, a blackbird came in through the window in a great flutter of wings.

He perched on the sill and looked down at the mermaid and said, "I have carried this message to you a long

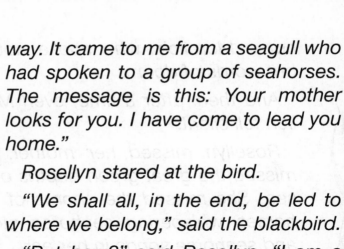

way. It came to me from a seagull who had spoken to a group of seahorses. The message is this: Your mother looks for you. I have come to lead you home."

Rosellyn stared at the bird.

"We shall all, in the end, be led to where we belong," said the blackbird.

"But how?" said Rosellyn. "I am a prisoner here."

"We shall all, in the end, find our way home," intoned the bird.

"How?" said Rosellyn.

"Ask," said the blackbird.

And then he flapped his wings and left the tower room through the narrow window.

The next day when the boy came to feed her, the mermaid turned and let him see her face. She spoke to him.

"Will you help me?" she said.

The boy was so surprised that he dropped the bowl he carried. "They said you could not speak."

"Will you help me? I want to go home."

"Where is your home?"

"I come from the sea," said Rosellyn.

"What is the sea?" asked the char boy.

And Rosellyn then described the sea for him — how the water changed from blue to green and back again, and how the sun shone through its great depths. She told him of the fish and the plants that grew there. She told him of the seahorses, and how they told story after story, each story more strange and wonderful than the last.

The boy said, "I would like to see this magical place."

"Will you help me?" asked Rosellyn. "Can you take me there?"

"Yes," said the boy.

Here, Beatryce fell silent.

She could hear the king breathing.

She could hear the distant weeping.

She could feel the beating of her own heart.

"And then what happens?" said the king. "You must tell me how the story ends."

"Must I?" said Beatryce.

278

Chapter Fifty-Two

They formed a procession. They marched through the great hall of the castle.

The goat came first, her head held up high.

Behind her was Jack Dory, and behind Jack Dory was Brother Edik, his hands in the sleeves of his robe, his wild eye rolling. He shouted, "I am bringing a prophecy for the king. Take me to the king!"

Cannoc followed them all, leaning on the cane, his face hidden, his steps shuffling and unsure.

The court musicians stopped their music. The noble ladies held their skirts up in both hands, afraid that the goat might brush against them. The men — the soldiers and the noblemen —

looked into the eyes of the goat and put their hands upon their swords, preparing themselves for warfare.

There was a tense silence in the castle.

Answelica's hooves, as they hit the stones of the castle floor, made the only sound.

"I have within me all the words, every word, of the Chronicles of Sorrowing!" shouted Brother Edik. "Take me to the king! I have a prophecy he must hear!"

Brother Edik was enjoying himself tremendously. He had never before so relished his strangeness, his wild eye.

Look at me now, Father, thought Brother Edik. *See who I am.*

The people parted. The four of them entered the throne room.

But the king was not upon his throne. Instead, there stood before them a man in black robes.

"You say you have a prophecy?" said the man. He smiled a twisted smile. "A prophecy the king must hear? I myself would love to hear it. I am very fond of prophecies."

Brother Edik opened his mouth, ready

to say whatever words came to him, but Jack Dory stepped in front of him. "It is not this monk who bears news for the king," said Jack Dory. "It is the king himself, here before you. He is the prophecy in the flesh."

Jack Dory turned to Cannoc. "I am sorry, Cannoc, but you must now reveal who you are. For Beatryce."

Cannoc nodded sadly, as if he had known it would come to this. And then he unfolded himself and stood up straight. He looked around him. He said, "I am no beggar, nor do I have need of a cane, for I am King Ehrengard."

There was a great murmuring among the noblemen and ladies, among the soldiers and musicians.

"Ehrengard?" they said. "Ehrengard is dead."

"Has he come back from the dead?"

"Could it be so?"

The musicians started up a triumphal song and then let it trail away. The soldiers banged their swords against the stone floor.

The man in the black robes who stood

beside the throne shouted, "The man is an impostor! Imprison him!"

"I am no impostor," said Cannoc. He did not shout. He said the words wearily. "I am the king."

The musicians started their song again. The soldiers came and gathered around Cannoc. One of the older soldiers reached out and touched Cannoc's shoulder.

"Sire," he said. "King Ehrengard. I remember you well." He knelt down before Cannoc. "The true king has at last returned."

"He is nothing but a charlatan!" shouted the man in black robes.

As for Jack Dory, he was paying attention to the goat. She had her nose up in the air. She looked directly at him.

"Now," she said. "Follow me."

Jack Dory answered her aloud.

"Wherever you lead, light of my heart, river of my soul," he said to the goat. "Take me to her."

He followed the goat, and Brother Edik, having heard Jack Dory's words, followed the boy.

Chapter Fifty-Three

n the dungeon, the king said, "Tell me how the story ends."

But Beatryce did not speak.

The king and the girl sat together in silence.

The only sound was that of the far-off weeping.

"I will tell you the rest of the story if you answer a question for me," said Beatryce.

"You dare to bargain with a king?"

"Who weeps?" asked Beatryce. "Whose crying do we hear?"

"Your mother, Aslyn of Abelard, weeps," said the king. "Now, tell me the rest of the story. Tell me what becomes of the mermaid and the king."

Beatryce's heart was loud in her ears. It beat out two words over and over: *your mother, your mother.*

Your mother.

"Tell me," said the king. "How does it end?"

When the whole castle was asleep, the boy put the mermaid on his back. The seahorse was entwined in her hair. They went together down the twisting stairs and through the gilded hallways and over the drawbridge and into the dark woods.

The blackbird appeared from the trees and spoke two words: "This way."

They followed the bird. They went deeper into the dark woods and through them and came to a cliff. Beyond the cliff was the sea.

The sky was indigo, and the stars were just beginning to fade, and the boy and the blackbird and the mermaid stared together out at the purple light reflecting on the water.

"It's even more beautiful than you told me," said the boy.

With the mermaid in his arms, he made his way down the cliff to the sea, where, moving toward them through the dark waters, was another mermaid.

Rosellyn's mother.

Rosellyn leapt from the boy's arms into the sea.

Her mother swam to her, weeping, smiling.

The seahorses surrounded them as they embraced. The seahorses sang to them.

And one-eyed Morelich at last spoke again.

He said, "Home. We are home."

The boy stood at the water's edge.

"But where now should I go?" he called to the mermaid. "Where is a place for me? I cannot return to the castle. The king will never forgive me for what I have done."

Here, Beatryce fell silent.

"That is not the end, surely," said the king. "What happened to the boy? What happened to the king?"

Beatryce did not answer him.

She was listening.

She heard the clatter of hooves. And the high, sweet song of a bird — a bird singing a beautiful, sad song.

The king, too, listened.

"What is that?" said the king. "What bird sings?"

"It is not a bird," said Beatryce. "It is a boy. And also a goat. And I would wager that a monk is with them as well, and somewhere, too, a true king, a wise king."

She felt suddenly that her heart might lift her up right out of the dungeon.

She did not feel imprisoned at all.

"They have come for me," said Beatryce. "They are here to take me home."

And then she called out, "Answelica! I am here! Here!"

Chapter Fifty-Four

ould Answelica open the lock on a dungeon cell?

Of course she could.

Her head, after all, was as hard as rock. And truly, what was a rusty lock compared to her love for Beatryce?

It was nothing at all.

It was naught, as Jack Dory would say.

Jack Dory and Brother Edik kicked at the door, and Answelica knocked her head against the lock of the cell until it had no choice but to give way.

They crowded into the cell with her.

Beatryce knelt down and opened her arms to the goat.

Brother Edik put his hand on Beatryce's head.

Jack Dory said, "Ah, Beatryce. There you are. I have come to learn my letters."

She smiled at him. "This is the second time you have come and rescued me from a dark room, Jack Dory. And you already know your letters."

"Aye," said Jack Dory. "And now I would like to learn to form them into words."

"I will teach you," said Beatryce.

"But how does the story end?" said the king.

Beatryce drew herself up and looked the king in the eye. She said, "The counselor you rely upon is an evil liar. And you are nothing but a fool."

She took the candle from the king's hand just before Answelica head-butted the man from behind, sending him flying through the air.

And then Beatryce shouted one word: "Mother!"

There came a strangled cry.

"This way," said Beatryce. She held the candle, and Jack Dory and Brother Edik and Answelica followed her.

They found Beatryce's mother in a cell, her mouth gagged, her hands bound. Answelica, with her hard head, made short work of the lock on that door, too.

Beatryce undid the gag on her mother's mouth and the rope on her mother's wrists. She wept as she worked. Her mother wept, too.

"Beatryce," said her mother when at last she could speak. "I could hear you. I could hear you the whole time. And I, too, want to know how the story ends."

Beatryce threw herself into her mother's arms. "This way," said Beatryce. "This is how the story ends."

BOOK
THE
LAST

ing Ehrengard ruled wisely for one full day.

Within that day, he exiled both the foolish king and his scheming counselor.

He sent the two of them far out to sea in an impossibly small boat with no sail and no oars.

"Go and tell lies to each other for all eternity," said King Ehrengard. "That is my punishment for you."

When they were gone, when the two men had disappeared from sight, King Ehrengard sat slumped in his throne. "I cannot bear it," he said. "I have no appetite for vengeance and no wish to be king."

Beatryce said, "Then why not walk away?"

"I have done that once," said the king.

"Yes," said Beatryce. "And now you have been given a chance to become the king who walked away twice."

King Ehrengard looked at Beatryce. He sat up straight, and then he threw back his head and laughed.

"Cannoc," said Beatryce to the laughing king, "did you not once say that it is perhaps time for a queen? I know of a wise woman who could rule well."

And so it was that Aslyn of Abelard was summoned to the throne room.

"Lady Abelard," said the king, "you are a noblewoman who wanted your children to be learned. You had the foresight and the courage to educate Beatryce. Beatryce is too young to be queen. She does not want the crown, in any case. But she believes, and so do I, that you have the wisdom and the fearlessness to lead. Will you take this crown from me?"

Aslyn said, "I will take this crown. I will take it to honor Asop and Rowan and Beatryce. I will do it for my children."

And so there now sits a queen upon the throne.

To the right of the queen sits Cannoc. He advises her on all things.

His beard has almost reached his feet. He laughs often. He looks closely at every face.

He listens well.

But he does not rule.

It is Aslyn of Abelard who rules.

It is Aslyn of Abelard, mother of Beatryce and Asop and Rowan, who rules wisely and well.

nd Beatryce?

She stands on a cliff with the great green sea before her.

Jack Dory stands to the left of her and Answelica to the right of her.

Beatryce rests her hand on the goat's head.

The girl and the boy and the goat all look out to sea.

"And so, by royal decree of Queen Aslyn, we three will go out into the land and teach the people to read," says Jack Dory.

"All the people," says Beatryce.

"All the people," says Jack Dory, smiling.

The wind blows Beatryce's hair around her face.

She can see far out to sea, very far.

And she is smiling, too.

nd in the dark woods, snug inside the trunk of a tree, Brother Edik bends over a manuscript.

He is drawing a mermaid with a bejeweled tail. He is drawing a seahorse with one eye. He is drawing a char boy and a blackbird and a king.

He is illuminating the world of Beatryce's story.

He is making a book.

He writes the words that end the story:

The mermaid looked down and saw that the jewels on her tail were returning. One after the other, they appeared.
    Rosellyn laughed aloud to see it.

A bee buzzes around Brother Edik's head.

He hums as he works.

"You will find your way home," said the mermaid to the boy. "Here, take this ruby; take this sapphire. I give them both to you with my whole heart, for you are beloved, beloved of me."

ll of this happened long ago.

Or perhaps it has yet to happen.

It could be that this book, the book of Beatryce, is the story of a world yet to come.

Who can say?

One thing is certain, though: what matters in the end is not prophecies.

Ask Brother Edik if that is not so.

What does, then, change the world?

If the hardheaded goat Answelica could speak, she would answer with one word: "Love."

And if you were to ask Beatryce of Abelard?

She, too, would answer "Love."
Love, and also stories.

ABOUT THE AUTHOR

Kate DiCamillo is one of America's most revered storytellers. She is a former National Ambassador for Young People's Literature and a two-time Newbery Medalist. Born in Philadelphia, she grew up in Florida and now lives in Minneapolis.

Sophie Blackall is the acclaimed illustrator of more than forty-five books for young readers and a two-time Caldecott Medalist. Born and raised in Australia, she now lives in Brooklyn.

The employees of Thorndike Press hope you have enjoyed this Large Print book. All our Thorndike, Wheeler, and Kennebec Large Print titles are designed for easy reading, and all our books are made to last. Other Thorndike Press Large Print books are available at your library, through selected bookstores, or directly from us.

For information about titles, please call:
(800) 223-1244

or visit our website at:
http://gale.cengage.com/thorndike

To share your comments, please write:
Publisher
Thorndike Press
10 Water St., Suite 310
Waterville, ME 04901